Granite

Graphite

Harzburgite

Heliotrope

Hematite

Hutchinsonite

Jadeite

Jasper

Kimberlite

Labradorite

Lapis Lazuli

Lherzolite

Limestone

Malachite

Marble

Mercury

Mica

Moon

sidian

Opal

Pegmatite

Peridot

Plagioclase

Pumice

Pyrite

Pyroxene

Quartz

Ruby

Sapphire

Serpentine

Shale

Silver

Skarn

Slate

Snowflake
Obsidian

Stibnite

Sunstone

Sulfur

Syenite

Tiger's Eye

Topaz

Torbernite

Tourmaline

Turquoise

Wehrlite

Wulfenite

Zincite

HIDDEN GEMS

Quest for the
Great Diamond

HIDDEN GEMS

Quest for the
Great Diamond

By
Hagop Kane Boughazian

Illustrations by Joel Sigua
Cover Illustration by Joel Sigua & Bea Castillo
Glossary Illustrations by Josh Lockwood

**GREAT
DIAMOND**

Text copyright © 2019 Hagop Kane Boughazian
Illustrations by Joel Sigua
Cover Illustration by Joel Sigua and Bea Castillo
Glossary Illustrations by Josh Lockwood
Illustrations copyright © 2019 Great Diamond Press, llc.
Cover Design by Gretchen Harwood

Printed in the United States of America
Library of Congress Control Number:2019909626

ISBN 978-1-7329276-1-2

10 9 8 7 6 5 4 3 2 1
First Edition

For my little ruby and moonstone.

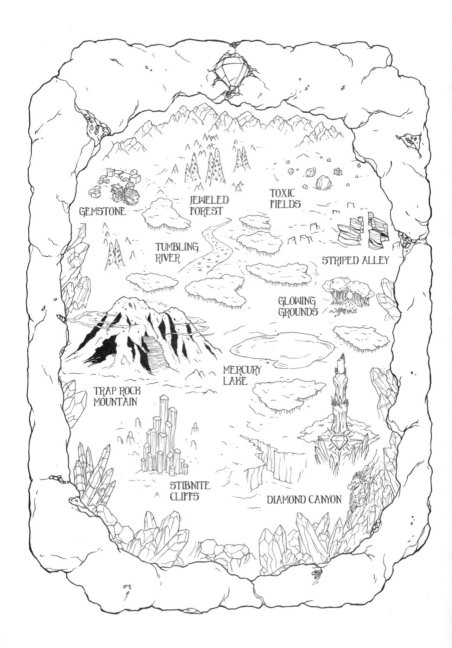

GEMSTONE

JEWELED
FOREST

TOXIC
FIELDS

TUMBLING
RIVER

STRIPED ALLEY

GLOWING
GROUNDS

MERCURY
LAKE

TRAP ROCK
MOUNTAIN

STIBNITE
CLIFFS

DIAMOND CANYON

Table of Contents

Prologue   1

Best Friends   4

Worst Enemies   8

Outcasts   12

Into the Jeweled Forest   14

Unexpected Adventure   19

The Great Diamond   25

Fact or Fiction   30

A Hidden Story   33

Home Alone   36

A Promise to Return   38

Embarking on a Quest   41

Stinky Encounter   45

Tumble Away   48

Dinner Party   53

You Don't Belong Here   59

Don't Run   66

Welcome My Child   70

Bedtime Story   76

A Risky Race   81

Rockslide and Roll   85

Captivating Queen   91

Pieces of You   98

Everything Falls Apart   101

Tears for a Friend   106

Dead End   112

Diamond in the Rough   117

Hidden Gems   121

Knowledge Will Set You Free   125

The Flight Home   132

A Long Story   137

"It's hard being a rock."

Prologue

The warm sun burst through the morning fog, stirring the wondrous creatures of the Jeweled Forest. The damp air buzzed with yellow topaz bees as they twinkled in the scattered light. Lime-green peridot rockhoppers fluttered around dew-filled garnet flowers. And lapis lazuli butterflies waited patiently as the sun warmed their deep blue wings, permitting them to lift their heavy pebble bodies into the sky. In the shadows of the tall malachite-covered trees, jadeite frogs sat atop wet moss, their long tongues snatching fast-flying jeweled snacks. Even the great bornite cranes were awake, singing their mornings songs as the sun scattered off their massive iridescent bodies. The entire forest seemed to be alive with colorful rocks and minerals. And right on the edge of this spectacular forest was a village filled with even more amazing inhabitants. The village was called Gemstone.

As the day began in Gemstone, rock families of all shapes and colors emerged from their sturdy yet humble homes. Rock parents hastily ushered their rock kids off to rock schools, promising them a wonderful day ahead. A cream-colored limestone father waved goodbye to his limestone son, who hurried off to join his sedimentary friends. A gray-and-white speckled young syenite woman greeted her rock neighbors as she went about her daily morning jog. And a colorful labradorite dog pulled its slate owner as it chased after a pegmatite squirrel. Dark obsidian families, gray shale families, and rough granite families all rushed to get to their rocky destinations.

And just as the rocks began their day, so did the minerals. Mineral families of all shades of the rainbow left their magnificently adorned homes. A citrine mother kissed her citrine daughter's shiny orange forehead and sent her off to mineral school. A purple-

and-green fluorite father rushed out of his house, late to his mineral job. And a pair of old topaz ladies walked through the park, lamenting the hectic pace of mineral life these days.

But even though these rocks and minerals lived together in one village, they led separate lives. Rock parents only worked in rock businesses and sent their rock kids to rock schools. And mineral parents only worked mineral jobs and sent their mineral kids to mineral schools. The rocks didn't want anything to do with the minerals, and the minerals didn't want anything to do with the rocks. Both sides found comfort in their separate identities and believed that they were too different ever to get along.

The last thing any mineral family could have imagined was having a child that was born a rock. But that is precisely what happened to Mr. and Mrs. Quartz.

Best Friends

I'm Gem, queen of the minerals!" Gem leaped up onto her pink bed. Her purple hair was piled up, poorly mimicking the crystals atop her mom's head. She raised her jewel-studded hairbrush in the air, pretending it was her royal scepter. The golden evening light from her bedroom window bounced off the jewels and scattered across the lavender room, blinding her friend Marble.

"You look more like the queen of crazy," said Marble as she hopped up next to Gem and seized the brush. They giggled as they flopped down onto Gem's bed.

Marble was Gem's classmate at Granite Elementary School and Gem's best friend. She was a tiny girl with smooth white skin, snow-white pigtails, and pale gray eyes. Her ghostly appearance frightened some of the other kids, but not Gem. Gem appreciated the fact that Marble was different, just like her.

Although Gem went to Granite Elementary, a school for rock kids, she was, in fact, the child of mineral parents—a secret she kept from everyone at school except Marble.

"Are you girls behaving in there?" asked Mrs. Quartz as she wedged her head through the narrow slit in the door. The purple amethyst crystals on her head sparkled in the light as they framed her slender face.

"Yes, Mom," said Gem, sounding annoyed.

"Marble, your parents should be here soon to pick you up," Gem's mom said as she shut the door.

"Your mom is so pretty!" exclaimed Marble. "She's so—"

"Purple?" said Gem, cutting her friend off. The two girls collapsed into a fit of giggles.

Gem pulled Marble up onto the bed. The two girls stared at their reflections in the mirror over Gem's dresser. "I wish I looked like her, like a mineral," said Gem longingly.

"Hey, what's wrong with looking like a rock?" asked Marble, placing her hands on her hips.

"Nothing," replied Gem, "if you're a rock. But I'm a mineral, I think. And look at me."

Gem wasn't a beautiful rich-purple amethyst like her mom, or a clear and shiny quartz like her dad. Instead, she was a dull, rough, grayish rock. Her purple eyes and hair were her only resemblances to her mother.

"I don't care what your parents are, you're a rock to me." Marble gave Gem a big hug. "And besides, you do go to a rock school. From what you've told me about mineral school, I don't know why anyone would want to be a mineral."

Gem looked at the scar on her shoulder in the mirror. Her experience at Granite Elementary so far had been much better than what she had experienced at Mineral Elementary—the all-mineral school.

At Mineral Elementary, Gem's rough gray appearance was a blemish in an otherwise sparkling sea of mineral kids. Her old classmates were red garnets, shiny silvers, orange citrines, and a whole variety of other minerals that sparkled like jewels. At Mineral Elementary, Gem was the target of much ridicule, especially from Emerald—the little green girl who had made life miserable for Gem, turning the entire school against her. Emerald was also the mineral Gem blamed for the scar on her shoulder, and for making her never want to go back to mineral school again.

No, all that was in the past now. Things at Granite Elementary were much better for Gem. Transferring her to a rock school was the best decision Gem's parents could have made, even if they hadn't liked the idea originally. Gem finally felt like she belonged, especially after making friends with Marble.

Gem and Marble were inseparable. They spent all their free time together. For Gem, any time with Marble was special. But their favorite thing to do was to sneak off into the forbidden Jeweled Forest.

The Jeweled Forest was off limits to the villagers and therefore the perfect place for Gem and Marble to escape. They never went far, just walked along the border next to the village, but that was far enough to be away from everyone else. With no one else around, Gem and Marble were free to be themselves.

With Marble as her best friend, Gem even forgot at times that she was different at all. For the most part, the rock kids had accepted Gem as one of their own. But then, one summer, everything changed.

Worst Enemies

O uch!" shouted Mr. Quartz as the pink soccer ball bounced off his head. Gem peeked out of her second-story bedroom window, her long purple-and-pink hair up in a ponytail.

"Oops! Sorry, Dad."

"Come on, Gem; Marble is here. You don't want to be late for your first game of the summer," said Mr. Quartz as he watered the freshly mowed brochantite lawn.

"Hi, Marble!" shouted Gem from her window.

"Hey, Gemmie!" replied Marble.

Gem ran down in a flash, her pink fluorescent hoodie flapping over a dark tank top and rich purple shorts. She had fully embraced the sporty look. The two girls hugged like they hadn't seen each other in ages.

"Have fun at the game," said Mr. Quartz as he waved the two of them off.

"I'll race you," said Gem. And before Marble could respond, Gem sped away.

"Hey! Wait for me," yelled Marble as she bolted after her friend. They ran through side streets and alleyways and jumped over small fences and obstacles. Gem loved the rush of running; it made her feel free.

"Hey, slow down," called Marble as she started to fall behind. "WE'RE NOT RACING!" she yelled.

"Come on, you can catch me," said Gem, encouraging Marble to keep up. Finally, they were at their destination, both girls completely out of breath.

"Hey, you have to let me win one day," said Marble.

"Not a chance," said Gem. "You're just going to have to try harder."

The sign outside the field read, "Granite Elementary School—Home of the Rock Stars." A group of rock girls wearing soccer jerseys with Rock Stars written on them were warming up at one end of the field. On the other end, a group of mineral girls prepared to play as well. The rusty bleachers were mostly empty except for a few parents and a handful of bored-looking kids. Marble and Gem slipped on their Rock Stars jerseys and joined their teammates.

"Let's crush these minerals!" said Marble as her teammates cheered. The Rock Stars had been playing soccer for a while, but only in all-rock leagues. Today was the first time they were playing a mineral team.

"You nervous?" asked Marble.

"No way, we've got this," said Gem.

Gem was exceptional at soccer. As the game began, it was clear that she was the quickest one on her team. She zipped around the field with the ball glued to her feet. As hard as they tried, no one from the mineral team could catch her. She ran the ball all the way across the field and scored a goal, right through the legs of a bright green girl. Gem and Marble high-fived as they celebrated. But their celebration was cut short.

"Hey, Rock Face! Remember me? I see you found where you belong." Gem's heart dropped at the sound of the girl's voice. It belonged to Emerald, the same girl that started all the trouble for Gem at mineral school. Emerald and her mineral teammates laughed as Gem walked back to her team.

"Hey, you okay?" asked Marble.

"Yeah. She's just trying to get in my head," replied Gem. Then Gem turned to the minerals and yelled, "I guess they're just afraid of losing!"

"Do you know that mineral, Gem?" asked one of the rock girls on Gem's team. Emerald overheard the question.

"Oh, you don't know?" said Emerald as she walked over to stand next to Gem. "Gem here used to think she was a mineral. She even tried to come to our school. Isn't that right, Gem?"

Gem felt anxious. Memories of mineral school raced through her mind. She remembered how Emerald made fun of her and gave her the nickname "Rock Face". She also remembered how Emerald provoked the little zincite boy to throw a rock at her. That rock cut into Gem's shoulder, giving her a scar. She thought that those days were behind her, but now they stared her in the face.

"Is that true?" asked another one of the rock girls.

Gem was in a daze.

"Yeah, but—" Gem tried to explain, but before she could start, Emerald stepped in.

"Don't you know? Her parents are minerals." All of Gem's teammates looked at Gem in disbelief.

"Come on, girls! Don't listen to her," said Marble as she pulled Gem away. But Gem could hear the other girls whispering to each other as Emerald walked away. The game continued, but Gem had a sinking feeling inside.

Outcasts

Three young figures were sitting at the top of the bleachers, watching the game. The one with jet-black skin, torn jeans, and a beanie stared intently at the game, mesmerized. His name was Obsidian. The other two were Opal and Pyrite. Opal was an orange, yellow, and green luminescent girl with two puffs of hair and an attitude that she wore in her outfit. And Pyrite was a bright and shiny guy with loud clothes and a loose style.

Opal and Pyrite were less interested in the game and more interested in figuring out what Obsidian was so intrigued by. Though Opal and Pyrite went to mineral school and Obsidian was a rock and went to rock school, the three of them hung out together, as they each felt like outcasts.

"Just look at her go!" said Obsidian.

"Who?" asked Pyrite.

Opal followed Obsidian's gaze to the rock girl with a purple ponytail.

"Isn't she amazing?" asked Obsidian. Then he added, "At soccer. She's amazing at soccer."

But Opal wasn't buying it. "You need help."

Then Pyrite leaned over toward Obsidian. He balanced himself on the bleacher in front of his friend. "Wait, are you?" He looked at Opal. "Is he?" Then he turned back to Obsidian. "No way! Obsidian has a crush on—"

Before Pyrite could finish his sentence, Obsidian jerked his leg away causing Pyrite to lose his balance and tumble down the bleachers.

"Oomf. Ouch! Uh. Owe!" Pyrite rolled all the way to the bottom of the bleachers. "I'm good!" he called out.

"Who is she?" asked Opal now that it was just her and Obsidian.

Obsidian took a deep breath. "Gem."

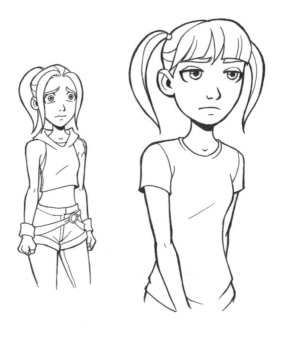

Into the Jeweled Forest

Nothing was the same after that game. Gem went from seeing Marble almost every day to seeing her twice a week, to seeing her once a week, and eventually to only seeing her on game days. At first, Gem thought it was just the usual summer stuff like vacations and camps, but after a couple of weeks, she started to suspect it was something else.

One day while Gem was out for a run she bumped

into Marble.

Marble was walking with a group of her Rock Star teammates, and Gem jogged over to join them.

"Hey, Marble!" Gem said, excited to see her friend.

"Hey, what's up Gem?" asked Marble.

Gem thought it was unusual that Marble didn't call her by her usual nickname. She wanted to ask why Marble had not been around, but not in front of the Rock Stars. Ever since they found out Gem had mineral parents, things had been different between her and her teammates. Now she wondered if the same was true for herself and Marble.

"Want to go for a walk?" asked Gem.

"Sure," replied Marble. Gem noticed her teammates didn't look happy to see Marble walk off with her.

"Let's go to the Jeweled Forest. It's been forever since we've gone there," said Gem, excited to get away and spend time with her friend.

"Don't you think we're a little old to be wandering in the forest still? What if we got caught?" replied Marble.

"How about you come over, then?" asked Gem. But Marble didn't seem to want to do that either. Then Gem finally came out and said what she was thinking.

"What's going on, Marble? Why have you been ignoring me?" Her heart raced.

"What? What are you talking about?" replied Marble, trying to sound surprised. But Gem could tell

Marble knew exactly what she meant.

"Come on, Marble. You've been ignoring me all summer. Ever since that game against the minerals. What happened?"

Marble didn't know what to say. "I'm sorry, Gem. It's complicated."

But Gem wasn't going to let it go. "Is it because of Emerald? You always knew about my parents, so what changed?" Gem kept pushing Marble for an answer.

Finally, Marble conceded. "Everyone knows now—so it's different." Then the words fell out of Marble's mouth like boulders. "I'm sorry, Gem, I can't hang out with you anymore."

Marble walked away, leaving Gem alone. Gem was too shocked to know what to say or do.

Gem remembered how she felt when she was little and the zincite boy had thrown a rock at her and scarred her shoulder. The pain she felt at this moment was even worse. Gem began to cry. How was she going to face everyone at rock school now, and with classes starting again in less than a week? She worried that it was going to be like mineral school all over again.

She had to get out of there. She pulled her hood onto her head and took off running as her mind flooded with dreadful memories. Images of her childhood chased her, and sounds of mineral kids laughing drowned the wind in her hair. Every name she was called and every dirty look she was given pressed against her chest making it hard to breathe. As she ran, she didn't think about where she would end up, and before she knew it, she had run all the way out of town and into the Jeweled Forest.

At least I can be alone here, she thought when she came to a stop just along the forest edge.

As soon as Gem stepped into the Jeweled Forest, a sense of calm came over her. She pulled down her hood and took a deep breath. The dappled rays from the sun broke through the mineral-covered trees and scattered colorful rays of light down onto her face. The warmth enveloped her as it absorbed into her body.

Gem started on her usual path—she had walked this path with Marble hundreds of times. She recognized the different rocks and minerals, each one marking a memory she had shared with Marble. First there was the turquoise pillar that Gem and Marble had carved their names into. Then she passed the red jasper flowers that Marble loved to pick and put in her hair. Next she saw the bloodstone under which they would hide secret messages for each other. And finally, she came upon the orange sunstone they sat on for hours, sharing details of their day. It all felt wrong being there on her own.

The memories felt painful, and Gem decided she needed to explore something new. Though she had never done it before, she walked off the path and headed further into the forest. At this point, she felt she had nothing to lose.

Gem wondered how she was going to face everyone back at school. Would she have to transfer schools again? Where would she go? Maybe her family would have to move out of Gemstone and find somewhere new to live. Gem wondered if there were other villages out there, past the Jeweled Forest. Maybe there was a village in which rocks and minerals lived side by side. A place where rocks and minerals went to the same schools; where they weren't judged as a group, but as individuals. The thought of that made Gem smile. She couldn't think of a time in her life when she didn't feel like an outcast for simply being who she was.

She was so tired of hiding, so tired of pretending to be something she wasn't. Whatever that was, she didn't even know. She looked like a rock, but never felt like one deep inside. And she felt sorry for her parents. Their mineral lives would have been perfect if she had been born a mineral.

Gem felt helpless as she wandered through the forest, lost in her thoughts. She was lonely, but though she didn't realize it, she wasn't alone.

Unexpected Adventure

Hey, look," whispered Obsidian. "Isn't that Gem?" Pyrite and Opal looked down from the granite ledge. The three of them had been stacking hoppers—little rocks with legs—to see who could balance the tallest tower. Building a tower of hoppers was much more challenging than using plain rocks, as hoppers used their legs to escape.

"Looks that way." Opal was annoyed. She had a gut

feeling that Gem was trouble for their trio.

"I wonder what she's doing here," said Obsidian. He had paused long enough for his hoppers to scatter away.

"Maybe she's lost," said Pyrite.

As Gem wandered by below, Obsidian tried to build up the courage to talk to her.

"I'm going to say hi," said Obsidian nervously.

"This should be fun to watch," said Pyrite with a grin.

As Obsidian stepped to the edge, he slipped off the ledge and landed right in front of Gem, startling her. Opal and Pyrite couldn't help but snicker quietly at him.

"Uh, hey," said Obsidian as he stood up and dusted himself off.

Gem stepped back. The stranger had surprised her. He looked about her age and somewhat familiar; she had seen someone wearing that obsidian arrowhead pendant in the hallways at school.

Obsidian realized that he might have alarmed her.

"Oh, sorry." There was an awkward pause. "Um, Gem, right?" he asked.

Gem was surprised. "How do you know my name?"

Obsidian tried to think of something to say that didn't make him sound like a weirdo. "Oh, I, um, I've seen you play. Soccer. You're a Rock Star, right?"

The Rock Stars were the last thing that Gem

wanted on her mind. "I guess," she said.

Obsidian noticed the change on Gem's face as he mentioned her team. "Are you okay?" he asked.

"Yeah, I'm fine," responded Gem untruthfully. She suddenly felt worried about the fact that she was alone with a stranger.

"I need to get back," she said, slowly stepping back from Obsidian. But as soon as she turned around, she bumped into Opal, who fell backward and slammed into Pyrite, who tripped on his flip-flops and wobbled a bit before falling into a sharp natrolite bush.

"Ouch!" yelled Pyrite as he jumped into the air.

"I'm sorry," said Gem. "I didn't see you there."

Pyrite pulled the white natrolite pins out of his shorts as Opal gave Gem a dirty look. Gem was surrounded.

"I'm Obsidian. These are my friends, Opal and Pyrite."

"A pleasure!" said Opal sarcastically as she crossed her arms.

Pyrite smiled proudly, holding natrolite pins in his hand.

But Gem wasn't in the mood to make new acquaintances. "I guess this place isn't as off limits as I thought," she said.

"That's why we come here. Because it's off limits and usually there's no one else around," explained Obsidian.

"We like the privacy," said Opal. "There aren't a lot of places where rocks and minerals can hang out together. That's why we're here—to get away from everyone." Opal looked at Gem as if to say that "everyone" included her as well.

Pyrite had become distracted by a lapis lazuli butterfly that was fluttering by. He reached up to grab it, much to Opal's displeasure.

"Don't touch it," she commanded. Opal didn't like anyone disturbing the beauty of the Jeweled Forest. She turned and looked right into Gem's eyes. "Looks like you're trying to get away from something too."

Gem realized she was tired of running. And tired of hiding. The one rock she could always trust, she could no longer call a friend. Without Marble, she had no one her age she could talk to. And this strange new girl in the forest could see right through her.

Opal saw the sadness form in Gem's eyes and felt sorry for what she had said. "I didn't mean to…" She said, unsure of how to finish.

Gem was fighting back the tears. She had nothing more to lose. "I just lost my only friend." She stared at Opal and Pyrite as she continued, with harsh blame in her voice. "You minerals, you've never liked me. Because of the way I look. Because you think I'm a rock." And then she turned to Obsidian, her voice rising. "And you rocks—you don't accept me either. Just because my parents are minerals." She began to cry. "Marble was the only one that accepted me, and now she's gone. I wish I knew why I was born different. Why I don't belong."

Gem wanted to shrivel up and disappear. But Opal, Pyrite, and Obsidian could all relate.

"Don't worry, we're all in the same boat," said Opal.

Her statement confused Pyrite. "What boat?" he whispered to Opal.

Opal just shook her head.

Gem calmed her crying. She glanced up toward the strangers that she had shared such harsh words with just minutes earlier.

"What do you mean?" asked Gem.

"I've never felt like a real rock either," said Obsidian. "I'm more like glass than rock. That's why some of the rocks make fun of me. They say that I'm going to shatter one day. And the rest of them don't even know I exist—like I'm invisible." Obsidian walked over to Opal and Pyrite. "If it weren't for these two, I'd have no one either."

Opal came over to Gem. "We all get judged. Just look at me. Everyone thinks I'm just a pretty face. They can't get past my beautiful, colorful, almost magical appearance." Obsidian looked perplexed at Opal's attempt to comfort Gem. "But I'm more than that…" Opal's voice trailed off.

Now Pyrite felt like he had to say something as well since everyone else had spoken up. "They call me fool's gold. Because my parents are rich, and, well, we're pyrites... doesn't make much sense to me."

Hearing all their stories made Gem feel a little better. She didn't realize there were others like her, who didn't fit in, who didn't belong. "Sometimes I wish there was a way to escape it all...all the glaring eyes and harsh whispers." Gem looked deep into the Jeweled Forest. "Have you guys ever gone out there? Further into the Jeweled Forest? I wonder what's past it."

"Nah, it's too spooky. This is as far as we go," replied Pyrite.

Gem stepped up onto a small granite boulder. "Maybe somewhere out there lies the answer to why I was born a rock," said Gem, "why I look like this." Then she stepped back down and sat on the rock. "Why couldn't I have been born a beautiful amethyst like my mom? Then everyone would accept me and stop treating me like some freak."

"Maybe you need to find the Great Diamond," Opal suggested. "He might have your answer."

The Great Diamond

Gem was intrigued. "Isn't the Great Diamond just a fictional character?" she asked. Gem's mom used to read her stories out of *The Adventures of the Great Diamond*, but those were just fairy tales. Or so Gem thought, until she spotted Opal's expression.

Opal sat down next to Gem. She unzipped her backpack and pulled out a sketchbook. The dusty-orange cover was creased and worn from use. But Opal didn't care how tattered her sketchbook looked. It was a gift from her mom, and she cherished it. As Opal flipped through the pages, Gem couldn't help noticing the detailed illustrations of rocks and minerals.

"Wow, these are amazing. Did you draw all these?" asked Gem.

"Sure did."

"How did you learn to draw like this?"

"My dad's an artist," replied Opal, as if that was a satisfactory answer. Opal continued, "I draw and write down info about every rock and mineral I see. I told you, I'm not just a pretty face."

Opal landed on a page with a shiny, handsome figure. "Here, have a look," she said. "Most people don't believe he's still alive, but I do. I drew this from an image my mom had."

Gem leaned over and looked at the drawing in Opal's sketchbook. She could see a striking figure with long flowing hair, and a chiseled face that looked strong and brave. Over the picture were Opal's notes:

The Great Diamond:

One of the greatest explorers and scientists ever to have studied rocks and minerals.

Knows everything.

Missing for decades. Believed to live beyond the Jeweled Forest. Exact location unknown.

Gem looked up at Opal. "What does that mean?

That he knows everything?" she asked.

"Well, just like it says. The Great Diamond knows everything. At least that's what my mom used to say," answered Opal. "No one has seen the Great Diamond in a long time, but I believe he's still out there, still working on his research, still uncovering the secrets of rocks and minerals."

Gem wondered if this Great Diamond could also uncover the mysteries behind her unusual appearance.

"Do you think I can find him?" asked Gem.

Opal paused and looked out into the forest. "The land beyond the Jeweled Forest is very large, and who knows the types of dangers that are out there?" Then she whispered, "But I do have a secret map that's supposed to lead to him."

"Can I see it?" asked Gem.

"Well, I don't have it on me. It's at my house," said Opal, starting to sound uncertain. "But I don't know how accurate it is. Plus, even with the map, it would be crazy to go out there."

"Or just desperate," said Gem. She thought for a moment. "I'm going to find him! Can I borrow your map?"

"Ummm." Opal thought about it for a second. She hadn't been fully truthful about her possession of the map. It was actually her mom's map, and she didn't really know where her mom had hidden it. Or if it actually led to the Great Diamond.

Listening intently to the girls, Obsidian could no longer stay quiet. "You can't go into the Jeweled Forest—not alone, at least," said Obsidian. "I'll go with you. We all will," he said, motioning to Opal and Pyrite.

Opal gave Obsidian a strange look. "We will?"

"You mean, like a quest?" asked Pyrite as he stuck his chest out and looked longingly into the forest. Pyrite had always wanted to go on a quest.

"Sure, a quest for the Great Diamond. If we all went together, we might have a better chance of finding him," said Obsidian. "Plus, Opal, you've been obsessed with the Great Diamond for, like, your whole life."

"I know, but—" Opal hesitated.

"No, it's fine. But thanks," interrupted Gem. "I can do this on my own. I don't want to put any of you in danger. Opal, can I borrow your map?"

Opal fell silent.

Pyrite was very excited about the possibility of going on an adventure. "I've got some questions of my own that I'd like to ask this Grand Diamond."

"Great Diamond," corrected Opal.

"That's what I said. Gr-r-r-reat Diamond. Plus, how dangerous can this forest be?"

They all looked out into the forest, except Pyrite, who walked off toward the trees with his chin up, as if trying to exude an air of bravery.

"What are you doing?" asked Obsidian.

"What? Wasn't that the line to start our journey?"

28

said Pyrite as he looked back.

"Remember, we need the map," said Opal. "If we're going to do this, we need to be ready."

"Best to get an early start tomorrow," suggested Obsidian. "Opal, you get the map, and we'll all meet back here at sunrise."

Gem was ready to go now, alone. But she did need the map. Reluctantly, she agreed.

Fact or Fiction

Gem slammed the door as she entered her house. "Everything alright, hun?" asked Mrs. Quartz, craning her head from the couch. Gem's mom was reading the latest issue of *Minerals Weekly*.

"Yeah, I'm fine," said Gem, hiding her true feelings. Gem plopped herself down.

"Hey, Mom, remember those stories you used to

read to me about the adventures of the Great Diamond? Were those stories real?" asked Gem. "Or is the Great Diamond a fairy tale?"

"Well, I don't know if all those stories are real, but the Great Diamond is no fairy tale," said Mrs. Quartz. "He's definitely a real mineral, though no one has seen him in a long time."

"And does he really know everything?" asked Gem.

Mrs. Quartz wondered why Gem had a sudden interest in the Great Diamond. "I don't know if he knows everything, but he definitely knows a lot about rocks and minerals." Gem's mom flipped through her magazine. "Some say he knows everything about every single rock and mineral, but I find that hard to believe. Why are you asking?"

"I just remembered the stories, but they are fuzzy. So what happened to him? Where did he go?" Gem was full of questions.

"Let's see," said Mrs. Quartz. "It's been a while. The Great Diamond was a scientist, a great scientist, and an adventurer. He would go on daring adventures into far off places and bring back rock and mineral specimens to add to the considerable collection in his lab. He studied them all and classified them."

Gem cut in. "What do you mean?" She hopped up and sat on the edge of the small copper coffee table, resting her chin on her knuckles.

"The Great Diamond wanted to know everything

he could about rocks and minerals, so he organized his collection into categories. Some say he's the one who gave every rock and mineral their name."

"So what happened?" asked Gem. "Did he finish his research?"

"No. One day while he was building a machine for his research, something went wrong. There was a big explosion, and the lab was destroyed. Some nearby minerals were even hurt. His entire collection was gone, and he was injured. Then, a few weeks later, he vanished. And no one's heard from him since."

"Do you think he's still alive?" asked Gem.

"I suppose so. Some say he left to go on his final adventure, and others say he gave up and went to go retire alone." Mrs. Quartz put down her magazine. "Why don't you go wash up. It's almost dinner time."

Gem felt excited. She wanted to believe Opal, but she just met her and didn't know if she could be trusted. But now, her mother had confirmed it was possible that the Great Diamond might be out there. Gem felt more determined than ever to find the Great Diamond.

A Hidden Story

When Opal entered her home, she soaked up the fresh smell of paint and the usual quiet of her house. Opal hardly noticed the comfortable hand-selected furniture that sat empty in the living room as she walked straight to her mom's office and slowly opened the squeaky door. The smell of the worn, dusty books and countless rolls of paper filled the room. The walls were covered with paintings by Mr. Opal, as well as framed photos of Mrs. Opal on her expeditions. Like the Great Diamond, Mrs. Opal was an explorer and scientist. The shelves in her office were adorned with an endless array of rock and mineral specimens. Opal loved them all and had become familiar with each one.

Opal knew that the map was somewhere in the office, but she had no idea where to look. The map was something her mom treasured, so it would likely be hidden carefully to keep it safe. Opal wasn't certain that she could find the map, or if it actually led to the Great Diamond, but she couldn't really show her face the next morning without it.

After searching for several hours, going through every book and filing cabinet in the office, Opal was ready to give up. "It's no use," she finally admitted. Her last effort was to ask her dad if he had any ideas for secret hiding spots. But she would have to be careful— she didn't want to reveal what she was looking for. Opal walked out of her mom's office and over to her dad's studio in the room across the hall.

"Hey, Dad," said Opal. He looked up from his canvas, covered in paint. There was no delineation between where the canvas ended and his clothes began.

"Hey, Opie," said her dad as he went back to his painting. His dark blue skin sparkled with fiery red bursts as he moved.

"I, um, I'm going on a little expedition tomorrow. Is

that cool?" asked Opal. "I won't be long."

"Sure, sure," responded her dad without looking up. He was focused on his painting. Even through the smeared mixture of orange and green, Opal could tell it was a painting of her mom.

Just as Opal was about to ask her dad if he knew of any good hiding places in her mom's office, it dawned on her. "The paintings!"

"What about the paintings?" asked her dad. But Opal was already gone.

She ran back to her mom's office and looked at the walls. *There!* she thought to herself. The largest painting in her office was a family portrait of Opal and her parents. Opal quickly grabbed the painting and pulled it down. As she opened the back, she saw it. The map! It was more spectacular than she remembered. "Yes!" she said as she rejoiced.

Opal slid the map into her sketchbook and ran back to her dad. She threw her arms around him and gave him a big good-night kiss. "Love you, Dad!" she said before rushing off to her room.

"Love you too," replied her dad. But again, Opal was already gone. "Huh, I wonder what's gotten into her."

Home Alone

P yrite walked up to the gate in front of his house and pressed the buzzer.

"Yes?" answered a voice.

"Hey, Beryl. It's me."

"Ah, little Pyrite. Welcome home," said Beryl as he buzzed the gates open.

Pyrite's house was a mansion, with gates and fountains and everything. Pyrite strolled past bushes in the front yard covered in rubies the size of apples.

He opened the front door and walked into the cavernous foyer. "Anyone home?" he called out.

"Just me, I'm afraid," said Beryl. Beryl had worked for the family for many years and cared a lot about Pyrite. "Your parents have gone on another trip. They won't be back for another four days."

Beryl's aquamarine eyes always gave Pyrite comfort.

"Okay. Thanks, Beryl," said Pyrite, a bit deflated.

Pyrite should've been used to his parents being gone by now. They had been taking trips to far-off destinations for years. He was too young to go with them when they started, but now he was older and still never got an invite. However, Pyrite's disappointment quickly vanished as he thought of his upcoming adventure. He would have a little trip of his own for once.

"Would you like some food, little Pyrite?"

Pyrite perked up. "Yes!" he exclaimed. "And, Beryl, can you pack me a backpack with some food and drinks for tomorrow? I'm going on a quest, and I need some supplies. And, Beryl, pack me a rope, a long rope."

"Do I dare ask what kind of 'quest,' little Pyrite?"

Pyrite thought about it. "Probably best not to."

A Promise to Return

Obsidian's house was the opposite of Pyrite's. It was tiny and plain. There was no gate, no buzzer, no fountain, no bushes with rubies. Obsidian pushed the unlocked door open.

All the curtains were drawn, making the living room darker than the evening sun suggested. Obsidian turned on the lights as he took off his beanie and tossed it on the small loveseat. It was the only seating his mom could fit into the small space.

"Obsidian!" called out a little voice excitedly. A tiny jet-black girl dotted with white snowflake patterns ran up and jumped on Obsidian.

"Hey, Snowflake," said Obsidian as he hugged his little sister. Snowflake was five years old and thought the world of her older brother.

"Hey, where's Mom?" he asked.

"Oh, she's taking a nap. She's very tired. Grading papers all day, you know?" said Snowflake. Obsidian knew she was mimicking what she had likely heard from her mom.

Obsidian's mom had been forced to go back to work after his dad left. At the same time, they moved from their bigger home to this one.

Mrs. Obsidian had left her teaching career when Obsidian was born. She kept up her skills by homeschooling him while she wasn't working, but the pace of working fulltime again and raising the two of them on her own was just too much. She always seemed to be tired.

Obsidian didn't understand why his dad had left. "He just lost his way," is all Mrs. Obsidian would say. Obsidian was still very young when it happened, right after his sister was born, so Obsidian didn't remember much about his father. The only thing he had from his father was the arrowhead pendant he had left behind.

Obsidian had made a commitment to his mom to

help her as much as possible, especially when it came to taking care of Snowflake.

"Okay, don't wake her up," said Obsidian. "Have you had dinner?"

"Yup! And I've brushed my teeth." Snowflake opened her mouth wide to show her brother.

"Great. I have a little favor to ask you. I'm going on a little trip tomorrow, leaving before mom gets up. Can you just let her know that I might be gone for a while?"

Snowflake looked sad. "You're coming back, right?"

"Of course. It might just be a day or two."

Snowflake started to tear up. "You promise, right?"

Obsidian gave his sister a big hug. "Don't worry. I'll be back before you know it. Just remember to tell Mom, okay?"

Snowflake agreed.

Embarking on a Quest

It was still dark out when Gem arrived at the meeting spot. She had never been in the Jeweled Forest this early in the morning. An eerie quiet filled the air, and a blanket of fog crept along the floor. But Gem wasn't scared. She enjoyed the peace and quiet. She sat down on a fallen log that was covered in red jasper flowers and looked out into the densely populated trees. She wondered what kinds of secrets they held, and if the Great Diamond would really know why she was born a rock. *There had to be a reason,* she thought. She couldn't just be a mistake.

The sun started to peek from behind the trees as the fog scurried away. Gem was doubtful that Obsidian, Opal, or Pyrite were going to show up. Minus the map, it didn't matter to her much either way—she was ready to set off on her own.

A rustling and then some footsteps cut the silence.

"Obsidian? Pyrite?" a voice called out. "Gem? Anyone?"

"Yeah, hi. Over here," replied Gem.

Opal came through the trees and walked over to Gem. She looked like she had woken up on the wrong side of the bed. "Where are the boys?"

"Not sure. You're the first one."

"Just like them, always slacking. They better get here soon, or I'm going back to bed." Opal leaned on a tree and shut her eyes. Apparently, she wasn't much of a morning mineral.

Gem picked one of the jasper flowers and looked at it closely. "I hope we find the Great Diamond quickly. I don't know how much longer I can go without knowing what's wrong with me."

"Ugh, nothing's wrong with you. You're just a rock," replied Opal. She turned to look at Gem more closely. "Probably basalt."

Gem slid the flower into her pocket. "Do you have

the map?"

"Sure do!" said Opal, sounding proud.

"Can I see it?" asked Gem anxiously.

Opal pulled the sketchbook from her backpack and flipped to the page holding the map. "Here it is!"

Gem reached out to grab it.

"Just be careful," Opal said, handing it over. "It's my mom's. She told me there is no other one like it."

The two girls looked over the map carefully as Opal read the descriptions, "Gemstone, Jeweled Forest, Tumbling River, Toxic Fields…"

"That doesn't sound pleasant," said Gem, cutting in.

"Can I finish?" commented Opal as she rolled her eyes, "Striped Alley, Glowing Grounds, Mercury Lake, Trap Rock Mountain, Stibnite Cliffs, and see, Diamond Canyon. That should be where the Great Diamond lives."

"Should be?" asked Gem.

"Well, has to be. Why else would it be called Diamond Canyon?" said Opal confidently. Opal and Gem were so engrossed in the map that they hadn't noticed the guys approach.

"So, is there a yellow brick road or something we're supposed to follow?" asked Pyrite as he squinted. The morning sun was too bright for him.

"You finally decided to show up," teased Opal. "We don't have a yellow brick road, but I have something better." She held the map high to show the boys.

"Whoa!" the boys gasped simultaneously.

"Let's see," said Opal, scanning the map. "Looks like we need to go through the Jeweled Forest and find the Tumbling River."

Stinky Encounter

Their journey into the Jeweled Forest had only just begun when the quiet and bare outskirts of the forest opened to a vibrant, wild, and lively world.

Gem couldn't resist rubbing her fingers on the malachite moss that covered the trees. And Pyrite stared at copper mushrooms growing under the shade.

"I wouldn't touch those," warned Obsidian. "They

might be poisonous." He dodged a couple of yellow tourmaline hummingbirds. They fluttered around him and then darted off to drink nectar from purple sapphire flowers.

The group strolled at an even pace, taking in the landscape. Opal was frantically sketching the tiny breccia lizards as they rushed around, disappearing in the dappled light of the forest.

"I never realized just how alive this forest was," said Gem. She looked up as metallic creatures swung from branches in the canopy high overhead. "Have you guys seen all this before?"

Gem turned and saw the mesmerized expression on everyone else's face. "I'll take that as a no," she said.

"If I had known how beautiful it was in here..." said Opal trailing off. Her pencil sat frozen in her sketchbook as she lost herself in the splendor that surrounded her.

"Uhhh, what's that smell?" asked Pyrite, covering his nose.

The strange yellow animals that were swinging on the tree branches had come down to visit the strangers in their forest.

"Well, it's probably these creatures," said Opal. "From the smell of it, I'd say they're sulfur monkeys."

One of the monkey-like creatures jumped right onto Pyrite's shoulder.

"I think he likes you, Pyrite," said Obsidian,

laughing.

"Ahh, get it off me! It smells so bad."

The creature rubbed its head on Pyrite's face while letting off a small yellow puff.

"I think you have a new friend," said Opal. She and Gem giggled.

Pyrite was not amused. "Shoo, shoo. Off me."

The sulfur monkey jumped off, but not before letting out another awful odor and a large yellow plume that clouded around Pyrite's head and seeped into his mouth.

Pyrite dashed around trying to escape the fumes and the rotten taste as the rest of the group just laughed at the sight.

"I'm going to puke!" yelled Pyrite. As he ran around hysterically, he suddenly heard splashing sounds from up ahead. "Water!" he exclaimed as he bolted off.

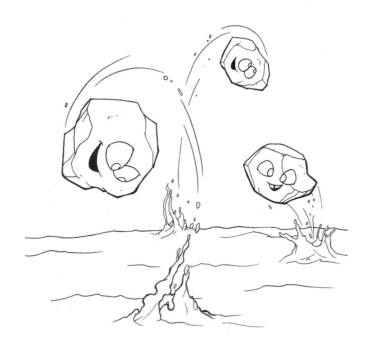

Tumble Away

The splashing was deafening as Pyrite arrived at the edge of a bright blue river. Hundreds of spherical rock creatures joyfully rolled, jumped, and flipped their way through the water. Their giant eyes swirled around making Pyrite dizzy.

Opal, Obsidian, and Gem soon caught up and witnessed the wondrous sight for themselves.

"What are these?" asked Pyrite in his loudest voice.

His gaze fixated on the rock acrobatics.

Opal, Gem, and Obsidian stood a bit further back from the river to avoid the spray in the air.

"Wow! I've never actually seen one," said Opal as she breathlessly fumbled around with her sketchbook. "I've only heard about them from my mom. They're called *tumblers*." She opened her sketchbook and began to draw.

The loud noise of the water and tumblers drowned out what Opal was saying. "What are these things called?" yelled Pyrite from the river's edge.

"Tumblers!" shouted Opal.

"What?" yelled Pyrite again.

"TUMBLERS! They're called tumblers!" screamed Opal in her loudest voice.

"Got it!" hollered Pyrite. "I bet this is the Tumbling River!"

They had found their next landmark on the map.

"Are they dangerous?" asked Obsidian.

"No, not at all!" said Opal loudly. She realized she was still shouting. "Sorry."

"They're adorable," said Gem. "But what are they doing?"

"Tumblers begin their lives up the river," said Opal. "They start as rough rocks, and they spend their entire lives tumbling down the rivers. By the time they reach the ocean, they are perfectly round and smooth."

"That's amazing!" Gem loved what she heard. She

thought it was wonderful that these creatures could change so much. It made her wonder if she could change too.

Gem walked over to Pyrite, who was now leaning over the edge of the river, trying to catch one of the tumblers. Obsidian walked over as well, while Opal continued to draw.

"Hey, be careful," said Obsidian. "You might fall in." And just as Obsidian spoke, Pyrite lost his footing on the wet ground. He wobbled back and forth, his arms flailing. Gem ran over to help, and Pyrite grabbed her with one hand and Obsidian with the other, trying to prevent himself from falling into the river.

Instead, however, he pulled them both down with him.

The three of them splashed into the shallow water as the tumblers rolled all around. A couple of the tumblers bounced off Pyrite's head.

"Ow! I thought you said they weren't dangerous!"

They all laughed.

"At least that smell is gone," said Gem.

Opal finished sketching the tumblers and slid her sketchbook back into her backpack. "Come on, let's keep going," she called out. But Pyrite, Obsidian, and Gem were all happy lying in a sunny spot, trying to get dry.

"Can't I just stay here?" whined Pyrite.

"Only if you want to make friends with that

serpentine snake there," said Opal, pointing toward a green spotted snake slithering next to Pyrite.

Pyrite and Obsidian sprang up in fear, but Gem just watched the serpentine snake slowly glide toward the edge of the river and take a sip. "It's just thirsty," said Gem.

"Well, we've found the Tumbling River," said Opal, looking at her map again. "Now we need to find the Toxic Fields."

Obsidian looked around. "That doesn't sound pleasant. And with all the strange plants and creatures in here, how will we know when we've found it?"

"Don't worry, we'll know!" exclaimed Gem. Her wet shoes squished as she rushed to join Opal. Obsidian and Pyrite followed the girls.

Gem seemed distracted as they walked through the dense plants. Opal could tell she was thinking of something, or someone.

"So, tell me about this Marble," inquired Opal.

Gem wasn't sure where to begin; just hearing Marble's name felt painful. She still couldn't believe that Marble had thrown their friendship away so effortlessly.

"She was my best friend. My only friend." Gem ran her fingers through the wet dangling strands of her hair. "She was the first one that spoke to me in rock school, first one that made me feel like I belonged." Gem bit her lip. "And when she found out that my parents were minerals, she didn't even care, and never told anyone else."

Gem chuckled at some of her memories. "She could never beat me in a race, as hard as she tried. I figured I'd have to let her win one day, but I never told her that. And just like the three of you, we would sneak out to the edge of the forest to get away from everyone else. I figured she understood me. But I guess she found what she was really looking for with the Rock Stars."

"I'm sorry. It sounds like she was a great friend." Opal let down her guard. "I've never had a friend like that. Never really fit in with any group," she admitted. Then she looked back at the boys. "These two weirdos are the only ones that seem to understand me."

"They don't seem that bad," responded Gem.

As they walked a bit further, the trees began to thin out. They could see unobstructed sky up ahead, and soon all the trees gave way to a spectacular open field covered in the most vibrantly colored minerals they had ever seen.

Dinner Party

That's definitely a field, but it doesn't look very toxic," said Pyrite. Wild jeweled minerals in a multitude of colors covered the field. Their bright saturated shades sparkled in the sun.

"I never imagined how beautiful it would be out here," said Gem, her eyes fixated on the bright colors.

They slowly made their way to the center of the field. Gem stroked her hand over the minerals, causing them to flicker and glow.

"Look!" said Gem excitedly.

"I don't like the way they look," said Obsidian.

"What? Why?" said Pyrite. "You really need to relax. I don't think anything in here is dangerous."

Pyrite bent down to get a closer look at a bright red mineral. He stuck his eye right up on it and looked through. "Whoa! Everything is red."

Just then, the mineral started to move, making Pyrite flinch. "Uh, I think this one just moved."

"What? Are you sure you didn't move it?" asked Obsidian.

"Hey, guys, um, I think they're all moving," said Opal.

They all watched as the entire mineral field began to sway.

"What are these things?" asked Gem.

"Don't look at me!" said Opal, raising her voice. The rustling of the minerals was getting louder and louder, letting out low rumbling sounds mixed with bright beeps and clicks.

"I thought you studied everything!" shouted Gem.

"Well, I've never seen these before!" Opal shouted back.

Then all the minerals started to blink; each one lit up in its unique color.

"Hey, maybe it's a party!" joked Pyrite.

As suddenly as the minerals had started moving

and blinking, they all stopped, going completely still.

"Aw, the party's over," Pyrite said.

Then all at once, the minerals opened their mouths to reveal sharp metal teeth.

"Apparently it's a dinner party," yelled Obsidian. "Run!"

"I don't want to be lunch!" cried Pyrite.

They raced through the field with the minerals gnashing at their ankles. The mineral creatures hopped around, jumping like fleas as they tried to bite the group. One of the creatures jumped up and bit Pyrite's shorts. "It bit me!" shouted Pyrite.

Obsidian grabbed a stick and swung it around knocking the creatures down.

Opal and Gem found themselves surrounded. They went back to back, kicking the creatures with swooping movements to keep them at bay.

Just as Pyrite was about to be in the clear, one of the creatures lunged toward him, pushing him into a nearby boulder. The contact created a large, bright spark that frightened the creature and made it run away. The others backed off too.

"What was that?" asked Obsidian. But Pyrite was just as puzzled as everyone else.

"Hit that boulder again," commanded Obsidian. And as Pyrite struck his arm against the boulder, more sparks flew, and more little creatures dashed off.

"Look, they're retreating!" said Gem.

"Do it again!" called Opal.

"Cool!" said Pyrite, surprised by his newfound ability.

Pyrite hit the boulder over and over, and each time a giant spark shot off his arm like a firework until all the creatures were off in the distance and the group was clear.

"I guess those creatures don't like fire," said Opal.

Pyrite looked down at his hands as if seeing them for the first time.

"Man, I can't believe I can create sparks! Why have I never noticed that before?"

"Maybe it's the type of rock you hit? Or how hard you hit them? Either way, it's pretty cool," said Opal. She patted Pyrite on the back and then examined the boulder he was hitting.

"I'm sorry, guys. I didn't mean to almost get you eaten," said Gem, "If you want to turn back, I won't blame you."

"We're the crazy ones for joining you," said Opal.

"It's my fault, I dragged you two along," said Obsidian to Opal and Pyrite.

"What are you guys talking about?" exclaimed Pyrite. "That was amazing! Sure, we almost died and all, but I learned I could make sparks! If we hadn't run into those creatures, I might never have learned that I have powers. Guys! I have powers! And you guys were awesome as well. We're an awesome team."

"I guess so," agreed Opal.

Pyrite started walking off ahead singing, "I didn't know, I had the spark in me! I never knew, of my abil-i-ty!"

"What are you doing?" asked Opal, quickly cutting him off.

"What, I thought I would…"

"Uh-uh. No way, we're not singing. This isn't an animated film."

They hadn't gone very far from where the mineral creatures attacked, when Obsidian noticed a thin ribbon of smoke in the distance.

"Guys, look over there," said Obsidian, pointing at the smoke. "Anything on your map about that smoke?" he asked sarcastically.

"Ha, ha. You're so funny," replied Opal.

"I think it's coming from a chimney. What if it's the Great Diamond?" said Gem, looking excited.

"No way. We haven't even made it halfway across the map," said Opal.

"Maybe we can ask for directions," added Pyrite.

Obsidian wasn't very pleased with the suggestion. "Sure, we'll just go knock on the door of some crazy mineral living in the forest and ask for directions to the Great Diamond," he joked. "Maybe they'll even give us a ride."

"A ride would be nice," said Pyrite, not grasping Obsidian's sarcasm.

After some squabbling, they decided they would investigate the smoke. They couldn't pass by without at least checking the place out. As they approached the house, the air filled with a delicious aroma.

"Mmmm, do you smell that?" asked Pyrite. "That crazy mineral sure knows how to cook!"

"Let's just be careful, okay?" said Obsidian.

The smoke was coming from the chimney of a small shack that looked very much at home in its surroundings. Mounds of dark gray hematite formed the blistered organic walls.

There was someone, or something, standing in front of the shed. It had its back turned and appeared to be tending to some creatures inside a pen.

As they got a little closer, Obsidian suddenly recognized the creatures.

"Hey, you!" shouted Obsidian. "Are these your creatures? They just tried to eat us back there!"

As the figure turned around, they were all taken aback by her alarming appearance.

You Don't Belong Here

The figure was an old lady. Her ancient face cracked and crumbled, battered by the sands of time. Her dull and dusty limestone head had a massive pale blue celestite crystal cutting right through the center, splitting her face in half. The celestite started at her nose and went all the way over the top of her head.

"Whoa!" said Pyrite as he hid behind Gem.

Obsidian wasn't as fazed by her appearance; he was too focused on the mineral creatures.

"Hello? Did you hear me? These creatures almost killed us back there."

The old lady moved slowly. "Creatures? What creatures? You mean my babies?" she asked.

"Those are her babies?" whispered Pyrite.

"They must've been hungry," said the old lady. Then she turned to the creatures. "Were you hungry? Did Mommy not give you enough to eat?" She spoke in a baby voice. Then she turned back to the group. "You must've been in their favorite lunch spot. You need to be more careful about where you go."

"Lunch spot? What lunch spot? We were just walking through the field," said Obsidian.

"The Toxic Field?" asked the old lady. She squinted at Obsidian, then looked closely at Gem, Opal, and Pyrite. "You don't belong here. No, no, no. You don't belong here at all. Now my babies—they belong here." She turned back to the creatures and continued speaking in a baby voice. "It's safe here for you, isn't it? Nothing to be afraid of here."

Pyrite wanted to get a better look at the mineral creatures, so he walked closer to the pen. All the creatures quickly huddled in the opposite corner, cowering in fear.

"Get away!" demanded the old lady. "You're scaring them!" She looked closely at Pyrite. "My babies don't like you. No, no, they don't like you at all."

"Excuse me," said Gem. Stepping between Pyrite and the old lady. "I'm Gem. This is Obsidian, Opal, and the one your creatures don't like is Pyrite."

"Ah, Pyrite. That explains it," said the old lady rubbing her fingers together. The crackling sounds they made sent chills down Pyrite's body.

"What are these creatures?" asked Gem, but the old lady didn't respond. "I mean, what are your babies?"

"My poor babies. They are banished minerals. Toxic minerals," said the old lady. Then she started to list their types, "Chalcanthites, hutchinsonites, torbernites, galenas, and the little red ones are cinnabars. All toxic, and all banished from the village. But they can't survive out here on their own, so I take care of them. It's not their fault they are toxic; they were born that way."

"Can I ask who you are?" asked Gem.

"Who, me? Ha! Just a crazy old lady who lives out here."

Obsidian looked to Pyrite as if to say, "I told you so."

"They used to call me Celest. But that was ages ago," added the old lady in a far-off kind of way.

"Can I ask you something, Celest?" said Gem, looking directly at the old lady's face. "Are you a rock or a mineral?"

"Ha!" chuckled Celest. "She can see me, right?" she asked Obsidian. Then she spoke to Gem, "I'm both, of course."

"I'm sorry, but I've never met anyone who was both."

"And now you have."

Gem continued with her questioning. "So why do you live out here?"

"I told you. Someone must care for these beautiful little sweeties," said Celest. "Plus, I never felt like I belonged in the village."

"I know how that feels," said Gem.

Celest continued, "I lived most of my life in the village, bouncing between the rocks and the minerals, never finding my place. I like it much better out here. No one judges you out here."

"But there *is* no one out here," said Pyrite.

"You're a bright one, aren't you?" commented Celest as she walked toward Pyrite. He sunk lower behind Gem. "So what are you kids doing out here? This isn't a safe place for children."

"We're on a quest to find the Great Diamond. I have a very important question to ask him," said Gem. "You wouldn't happen to know where to find him would you?"

"Great Diamond? I haven't heard that name in a long time." Celest looked displeased. "It's all his fault."

"What?" asked Gem.

"Nothing," answered Celest in a sharp voice. "I have no idea where he lives. You should go now. And be warned, my babies are the least of the dangers out there."

Her voice made Pyrite so afraid that he toppled over onto the ground.

"We'll be fine," said Gem as she picked Pyrite back up. "Thanks for your time. Where to next, Opal?"

Opal, who had been sketching Celest the entire time, put down her sketchbook and looked over her map. "Looks like we head toward Striped Alley," she said.

"But what about resting? What about that delicious smell?" complained Pyrite.

Obsidian, Opal, and Gem all gave him a dirty look.

"Fine. Let's go," said Pyrite, sounding defeated.

"I wonder what she meant by it's all his fault?" asked Gem as they walked away.

The land grew quiet as the sun started to slide back down toward the horizon. The heat lifted away as a cool breeze rushed through the tall striped rocks that shimmered in the setting sun. The light danced between the orange, brown, and black stripes on the rocks as the group passed by. Gem, Opal, Obsidian, and Pyrite quietly walked as they looked around for a place to stop for the night, marking their bearings against the map.

"Looks like we're entering Striped Alley," said Opal.

"They're pretty magnificent," commented Obsidian.

Gem found herself walking next to Pyrite.

"I still can't believe you have this amazing ability

you didn't know about," said Gem.

"I guess I don't know a lot about myself," said Pyrite.

"Can I ask why?" Gem said kindly.

Pyrite grabbed a stick off the ground and started twirling it in his hand. "I don't know." He paused for a second. "Sometimes I wonder if my parents are ashamed of being pyrites. Like it doesn't fit the image they have of themselves. And I don't fit that perfect image either. So why would I want to know more?"

"I'm sorry," said Gem.

"Whoa, that was deep," said Pyrite, reflecting on his words. He laughed it off. "It's fine. I don't really care." But his voice gave him away.

Then Pyrite closed his eyes and stood there completely frozen, in a state of suspended animation. The golden fading sun glistened off his shiny hair. Gem looked puzzled. She waited for him to do something, to say something. Then she snapped her fingers in front of Pyrite's face, trying to snap him out of it.

Pyrite finally opened one eye, then both eyes. "We're not cutting to a flashback?" he asked.

"We don't have time for that," replied Obsidian from up ahead. "Come on, we need to keep moving. It's getting dark."

The sun sank quicker and quicker into the distant horizon. The sky above was a deep blue, and the first few stars to wake up were sparkling above.

"I sure hope we don't run into any wulfenites!" said

Opal with a worried look. "I hear they roam in packs at night."

"Opal's right, we need to start worrying about what comes out at night," said Obsidian.

Pyrite stopped. "You mean, like a huge striped creature with orange pupils and sharp claws?" he asked.

"That's pretty specific," replied Obsidian. "But, sure, like that."

"No, not li...li...like...that," Pyrite stuttered as his outstretched finger pointed directly to a menacing creature in the distance. "Like *that*!"

Don't Run

The moonlight cast long shadows over the creature's face as it gracefully approached. Its orange eyes glowed with fire as light scattered through its striped body.

"Run!" shouted Obsidian. But Opal immediately put her arms out and stopped him.

"No! Don't run. Running doesn't solve everything. Besides, it'll chase us if we run," said Opal.

Then Pyrite had an idea. "Maybe we should climb on top of each other to make ourselves look bigger?"

"That's actually an excellent idea," replied Opal, impressed.

Pyrite clasped his hands together and lifted Obsidian up and onto his shoulders. As soon as Obsidian found his balance, Gem handed him two sticks.

"Here, hold these for me," she said.

Then Gem climbed over Obsidian, using him like a jungle gym, until she could stand on his shoulders.

Finally, Opal climbed up, stepping all over Pyrite, Obsidian, and Gem.

"Hey, watch it," complained Obsidian as Opal's boots pushed down on his face.

The tower was complete, but not very stable. They swayed back and forth like a blade of grass blowing in the wind.

"Give me the sticks," said Gem. She grabbed the sticks and waved them around like long arms.

The creature was approaching at a menacing speed when Pyrite started to howl. "*Awoooo!*"

They all howled together, making an awful sound, trying to scare the creature. But it was no use; the creature didn't look fazed by their antics.

Their stack started to sway more and more, and then suddenly it toppled over sending Opal, Gem, Obsidian, and Pyrite crashing to the ground.

"We're done for," said Pyrite as he curled up on the ground. The creature was so close that Pyrite could feel its breath on his face.

"Excuse me," said the creature in a soft and gentle voice.

"You can talk," said Opal, surprised. "How can you talk?"

"What kind of question is that?" asked the creature.

"Well, I, um, I didn't…" Opal trailed off.

"You didn't what? Expect a creature like me to be able to talk?"

"Well, yes," answered Opal honestly.

"Outsiders, always with their misconceptions. Don't be so deceived by appearances," said the creature, rolling its eyes.

"We're sorry," apologized Gem. "We were just scared."

Her words made the creature even more furious. "Wow! Adding insult to injury. So now I'm dumb *and* scary?"

"No, I didn't mean it like that. We've just never met anything like you before."

This statement seemed to please the creature. "There aren't many tiger's eyes like us left. We're pretty rare, you know. That's why I have to be so protective of them."

"Tiger's eye," said Opal in amazement.

"Mrs. Tiger's Eye," the creature responded.

Then Mrs. Tiger's Eye glided right between the group as she passed. As they turned around to see where she headed, it all made sense. Three cute tiger's eye cubs huddled in the bushes behind them. Mrs. Tiger's Eye wasn't trying to attack them. She was trying to get to her cubs.

"They're so cute!" said Pyrite. "Can I take one home for a pet?" he asked jokingly.

"Why don't you ask their mom?" replied Opal.

The four of them finally got off the ground and dusted themselves off.

"It was great meeting you, Mrs. Tiger's Eye. But we have to keep going if we're going to find the Great Diamond," said Gem.

"The Great Diamond?" said Mrs. Tiger's Eye, surprised. "Maybe you should head that way." She nodded toward a faint light in the distance.

Thanking Mrs. Tiger's Eye and catching one last glance at the young cubs, the group continued on their way in the darkness.

Welcome My Child

As night fell, they considered stopping for the night, but Obsidian had an idea. "Hey, Pyrite, can you make a spark?"

Pyrite grabbed a rock and struck it against his arm. A small spark jumped off his arm and landed on a pile of dry sticks that Obsidian held. The sticks immediately caught fire.

"Watch out!" screamed Gem as she saw the fire

reach Obsidian's arm. But he didn't even flinch.

"Don't you feel that?" Gem asked.

"What? I'm made of obsidian. Fire doesn't hurt me." Obsidian shrugged casually.

Relieved he wasn't hurt, Gem followed the glow of Obsidian's torch.

As they went further, the landscape changed. The tall striped rocks were replaced with densely packed trees. The stars and the moon hid behind the leaves, but a light came up from the ground in a mysterious fashion.

"Look! The ground is glowing," said Pyrite.

"We must be in the Glowing Grounds," said Opal. "But I don't think it's the ground that is glowing."

Scurrying around the forest bottom were thousands of tiny glowing mineral insects. "Not again!" sighed Pyrite, worried that they might be attacked like they had been with the toxic mineral creatures. But these beings weren't attacking.

The busy insects pulsed on and off in a rainbow of colors. Every time one of the kids took a step, the glowing mineral insects rushed out of the way like bright luminescent waves. The glowing mineral insects crawled up onto the trees, bushes, rocks, and flowers in search of food. Soon, the glowing lights were all around them. But up ahead, the brightest light source was glowing like a carnival.

"Look," said Gem. "What if it's the Great

Diamond?"

"You know how maps work, right?" asked Opal. "We still have a ways to go." But she was talking to no one, as Gem had already rushed ahead, spellbound by the sight.

Dozens of tall torches with glass jars surrounded the encampment. Inside each glass jar were hundreds of the glowing mineral insects, illuminating the jars from within. The colored lights from the mineral insects bled into each other creating a bright, warm glow.

Tall tapestries hung from long posts. Their patterns, depicting different rocks and minerals, were distorted as they blew in the wind. In the center of the tapestry ring was the most amazing sight—a glowing, floating figure. His legs were crossed in a seated pose, and his fingers pinched together as if he was meditating. He had long flowing braids in his hair, and his eyes were closed. Gem thought he looked a lot like the drawing in Opal's sketchbook.

He must be the Great Diamond, she thought, and she dashed toward him before anyone could stop her.

"Excuse me. Are you…" she could barely get the words out of her mouth "…the Great Diamond?"

"*Om*," the floating figure responded.

Gem wasn't sure if he had heard her, so she tried again. A little louder this time. "Hello? Are you the Great Diamond?"

The figure "*om*ed" again.

"He's not going to answer you. Not when he's in the zone," said a voice.

A bright red girl with glowing red eyes and a long flowery dress appeared before Gem. She wore a crown of flowers interspersed with glowing mineral insects in her long crimson hair.

"Ruby," she said, introducing herself. "But my friends call me Rubes." She offered her hand to Gem.

"Hi," said Gem. "I didn't see you there."

"That's okay. It's hard to get noticed over him!"

"I'm Gem," she said as her friends joined her. "And this is Pyrite, Obsidian, and…" Gem stopped cold, surprised to see Opal glowing in an assortment of fluorescent colors. "…Opal?" she continued with puzzlement in her voice.

Pyrite turned to Opal. "Um, why are you glowing?" he asked. But Opal didn't know either.

"It's the lights," said Ruby. "These lights make some minerals glow."

As impressive as a glowing Opal was, Gem was still more interested in finding out if the floating figure was the Great Diamond.

Gem turned to Ruby. "We're searching for the Great Diamond. I have something very important to ask him."

"Really?" said Ruby. "What's so important that you've come all the way out here to find the Great Diamond?"

Gem paused for a second. "It's…it's about me. I have to ask him why I was born different. Why I was born a rock, when my parents are minerals."

"That doesn't seem like such a big deal," said Ruby.

"Maybe not to you, but it's ruined my life," Gem said with conviction.

The floating figure opened his eyes and winked at Ruby.

"Then I present to you, the Great Diamond!" Ruby waved her arms in the direction of the floating figure.

"Welcome, my child!" he said in a super low voice. "What can I do for you?"

"I…I want to know why I'm a rock," said Gem.

"That's not so bad," he replied. His voice didn't sound as low this time.

"No, I wasn't finished." Gem looked into his pale sparkly eyes. "I want to know why I'm a rock when my parents are minerals."

He scratched his chin. "I see. Now that *is* a problem, isn't it? Maybe they're not your real parents. Maybe you were taken as a baby from your real parents and given to evil step-parents who made you work for them and do all the chores."

"What? No. My parents are not evil, and they are my real parents." Gem didn't think the Great Diamond was making much sense.

"I got it!" he exclaimed. "A curse has been put on you, and you have to find your true love to become a mineral again." He eyed Obsidian and Pyrite, suggesting that maybe Gem's true love was one of them.

"What are you talking about?" Gem was very confused and getting annoyed. "I wasn't cursed!"

Then the mysterious figure and Ruby burst into laughter.

"That was too good!" said Ruby.

"Did you see the look on her face?"

Gem was upset. "What are you two laughing at?"

Ruby and the floating figure composed themselves as their laughter grew quieter. "We're sorry. We couldn't resist. You had such a hopeful look on your face," said Ruby. Then she confessed, "This isn't the Great Diamond."

"Yeah, I figured," grumbled Gem.

Ruby continued. "This is my brother, Moonstone."

"Pleased to meet you," said Moonstone, but Gem wasn't very pleased at all. Neither were her friends.

"What's wrong with you?" said Opal, just as irritated as Gem.

Moonstone stepped down. As it turned out, he had not been floating. He was simply sitting on a tall platform.

"Don't be upset. We were just having a little fun. We get bored out here," said Moonstone. "Look, if you're looking for the Great Diamond, you're on the right path. But our father can be very elusive."

Then Gem, Opal, Pyrite, and Obsidian all responded simultaneously, "Your father?"

Bedtime Story

The group couldn't believe what they were hearing. Were these two really the Great Diamond's children? And were they finally getting close to finding the Great Diamond?

"Well, where is your father?" Opal demanded. "You owe us after that trick you just pulled." She wasn't about to show the strangers her map.

Ruby and Moonstone chuckled again. "We said

our father could be elusive. He keeps to himself. He doesn't even tell us the location of his secret lab."

Gem didn't know what to believe anymore. *How could a ruby and a moonstone be children of a diamond?* she wondered.

Obsidian looked up at the night sky, and then over to his tired-looking friends. He too was weary and ready to call it a night.

"Do you mind if we spend the night here?" Obsidian asked Ruby.

"Not at all. You can stay here as long as you like!" said Ruby as she straightened the flowers in her hair.

Moonstone and Ruby helped the group get their camp settled, and then they all gathered around a fire. "Do you guys like stories?" Moonstone asked.

"Oooh! I love stories," said Pyrite, excited.

Moonstone settled in and began his story. "Once upon a time, this planet was just a big molten hot soup."

"Mmmm, soup," interrupted Pyrite. Everyone stared. "What? I'm still hungry."

Moonstone handed Pyrite a small bowl of cloudy soup. "Have some of this," he said.

Pyrite took the bowl. And as he poked at the soup with his spoon, it began to spiral around.

"The fiery molten soup contained everything we see today. Rocks and minerals flowed freely, all connected. The world was one. Nothing had an identity, nothing had a name," said Moonstone.

Pyrite was watching the spiraling soup in his bowl when it suddenly solidified into different colored chunks.

"But as millions of years passed, the planet cooled. And everything separated. What was once connected, became separate. What was previously one, became many. And with that shift, the connection was lost."

Pyrite took a bite from one of the solidified cubes in the bowl. "It's good," he said with a mouthful.

"So I sit here on my platform, meditating, trying to find that connection again," said Moonstone. "It's what my dad told me to do. Said something about finding inner pieces, whatever that means."

Gem was trying hard to understand Moonstone's story, but it didn't really make sense to her. And she wasn't the only one—Obsidian and Opal looked toward Gem, unsure of how to respond to Moonstone's odd tale.

Meanwhile, the soup made Pyrite sleepy. After his first bite, he was nodding off on his blanket by the fire.

"We're off to bed," Ruby said abruptly. She got up with her brother, and the two headed off.

"What was that all about?" asked Obsidian.

"I don't know," said Opal. "I'm too tired to think."

"I think it was an allegory," said Gem. "It means we're all connected. But I don't know if I can believe anything those two say. Even if it were true, even if we were all connected once, that was a long time ago.

There doesn't seem to be any of that connection left."

"Do you think Pyrite's okay?" Opal asked.

Obsidian checked his friend, who seemed to be sleeping tightly. "He's just sleeping. I'm going to bed too," he said. He went off to his blanket leaving Gem and Opal alone around the fire.

Gem's mind was racing too much to fall asleep. Opal pulled out her sketchbook and began to draw by firelight. All the glowing mineral insects seemed to have stopped glowing.

"Who are you drawing? Moonstone or Ruby?" asked Gem, peering over her friends' shoulder.

"Neither," answered Opal.

Gem leaned over to get a closer look. "Who is that? She's beautiful."

"My mom. She's the most beautiful mineral I've ever seen, and the smartest as well. She knew everything about rocks and minerals and used to tell me all about them."

"Used to?" asked Gem nervously.

"Yes."

"I'm sorry," Gem said. She swallowed to speak but didn't know what else to say.

Opal chuckled. "She always wanted to find the Great Diamond. Just like you."

"Did she ever find him?" asked Gem, but she already knew the answer in her head.

"When you asked if we could find the Great

Diamond, I don't know…that set off something in my head. It was like a sign, a message, from my mom," Opal confessed.

"We found his kids. I know we'll find him," said Gem.

"I really hope so," said Opal.

Now Gem knew why Opal had told her about the Great Diamond, and why she had set them off on this journey. It wasn't for Gem; it was to finish something Opal's mom had started. Gem wanted to know more but didn't want to press her new friend. She knew what it was like to lose someone.

A Risky Race

Early the next morning, Gem and her crew left Moonstone and Ruby's camp to continue their journey. Several hours passed as they searched for signs of Mercury Lake, the next stop on the map. Before they left, Ruby warned them that the lake was very dangerous given that it was full of mercury. She recommended they keep their distance and go around.

The group had not heeded her warning, however,

and were well on their way. They were just beginning to think maybe the lake didn't exist, when suddenly they came over a hill to find it. Shining like a mirror in the hot midday sun, the reflection off the surface was blinding. Mercury Lake was calm and motionless. There were no waves or ripples, or any other motion on the surface. The lake was completely still.

"That's definitely a mercury lake," said Opal.

"Now that we've found it. What do we do?" asked Obsidian as he sat down on the beach next to the lake. The pebbles shifted under his weight.

"We cross it," said Gem optimistically.

"Where's that boat we're all in now?" mumbled Pyrite.

As he plopped down next to Obsidian, the impact sent pebbles floating. They rose up in the air around Pyrite as if they were weightless.

Opal knelt and picked up a handful of the pebbles. They felt weightless in her hand. She tossed them in the air, and the tiny pieces floated like dandelions in the wind. "Pumice," she said.

"Who?" asked Pyrite.

"No, not who—what. This is all pumice," said Opal, gesturing to the shoreline. "It's extremely light rock. I once heard of someone who was made of pumice— supposedly she could fly." Opal grabbed another handful of pebbles and tossed them toward the lake. They flew through the air before landing on the surface of Mercury Lake, where they stayed afloat.

"Cool. Are we going to fly across?" asked Pyrite.

Opal thought for a second. "Hmmm, we can't fly, but maybe we can float across the lake." Opal walked over to some giant boulders near the shore. "Hey, Gem, come pick one of these up."

Gem wasn't amused. "You're kidding, right?"

"Come on. Trust me," urged Opal.

Gem finally walked over to the boulders. "What do you want me to do?" she asked.

"Toss one in the lake."

"Seriously?"

"Just try."

Gem leaned over to grab one of the giant boulders, and before she knew it, she was lifting one over her head. The boulder was the size of a barrel. There was no way Gem should've been able to lift it up, but she did! Pyrite's and Obsidian's jaws dropped in disbelief.

"I knew it. These rocks are full of tiny holes that make them very light. And buoyant. Toss it in the lake," said Opal.

Gem tossed the boulder, and it landed on the surface of the lake without a splash.

"Come on, we can ride these across," said Opal.

"That's crazy," said Obsidian. "What if we fall in? Remember what Ruby said." Obsidian was having doubts about continuing the mission. He thought about returning home. He thought about Snowflake.

What would she do if something happened to him? If he never returned?

But Gem wasn't as doubtful. "Let's go!" she said as she grabbed another giant boulder and tossed it in the mercury. Then she got a running start and jumped right onto the floating rock. After a little wobble, she took a deep breath and started to walk. As she walked steadily, the boulder spun, moving her forward. "See, it's easy. All we have to do is walk, and the boulders will roll."

"Brilliant," said Opal as she jumped on a boulder herself. "But I bet we can get across faster if we run. I'll race you!"

Gem couldn't resist a race. "You're on!" And the two were off, zooming across the lake. "You guys better get going if you want to catch up," Gem called back to the boys.

Obsidian and Pyrite dusted themselves off and followed the girls' lead. Soon they were having so much fun, they forgot all about what would happen if they fell in. Good thing they never found out.

One by one they landed on the opposite shore of the lake, relieved not to have fallen in. But as they examined their new surroundings, their relief turned to worry as they faced the obstacle ahead.

Rockslide and Roll

O h, come on!" exclaimed Obsidian. "There's no
way we can go over this mountain."

Although they had successfully crossed
Mercury Lake, they were now at the base of an
enormous mountain. It was impossible to tell how high
the jagged rocks reached since the top was shrouded
within dark clouds.

"Well, this checks off another landmark," said Opal,

looking at her map. "We must be at the bottom of Trap Rock Mountain."

"Anyone know if there's an elevator?" asked Pyrite.

"Elevator? There's no elevator!" yelled Obsidian. The anger in his voice wiped the smile off Pyrite's face. "We'll have to turn back," Obsidian commanded.

"What? No way," said Gem defiantly. "I didn't come this far to turn back. We'll just have to climb."

"How?" questioned Obsidian. "It's a sheer wall, and we don't have any climbing equipment."

"There's got to be a way," said Gem as she searched the base of the mountain. "Opal, see if there is a way to climb on your side."

The two girls walked in opposite directions as they searched for any way to get up the mountain. They soon found what they were looking for.

"There! Look!" shouted Opal, just as eager to reach the top as Gem.

Obsidian, Gem, and Pyrite rushed over to Opal. She was staring at a portion of the mountain that was carved out, leaving behind surfaces that resembled terraces.

"Looks like someone, or something, was mining here. Wonder what they were looking for?" said Obsidian.

"Maybe they were just carving out steps for us to climb," said Gem sarcastically.

"So we're climbing?" asked Pyrite.

"Looks that way," complained Obsidian.

"Follow me," said Gem as she led the way.

Opal followed right behind her. Then Pyrite. And Obsidian went last to keep an eye on everyone. He knew he couldn't really do anything if someone slipped and fell, but it made him feel better anyway.

The rock on the mountain wasn't as sturdy as it looked. Pieces crumbled under their feet and rained down below. The higher they climbed, the looser the ground became. The air also changed, getting thinner as they ascended. The warmth of the sun was now masked by the cool clouds hanging off the side of the mountain.

After climbing for quite some time, the group paused to observe their location. Obsidian looked up and saw nothing but clouds, and looked down to find the same.

"I'm not sure we can go much further. This mountain might go on forever," he suggested.

"Seriously? Nothing goes on forever," said Gem. She was determined. "We have to keep going."

Pyrite saw a small ledge and plopped himself down. "Hey, guys, can we take a break?"

Gem could see that Opal and Obsidian looked tired as well. "Yeah, I guess so. But we're not turning back. At least, I'm not."

"Me either," said Opal, pumping herself back up.

"This feels nice," sighed Pyrite as he stretched his

toes.

Obsidian still didn't think climbing the mountain was such a good idea. "We don't want to be up here when it gets dark."

"Then we'll have to climb faster," said Gem as she started back up the mountain.

"I agree with Gem," Opal said, following suit.

"But the break…" Pyrite dragged himself back up as he knew it was no use trying to argue.

As Gem stepped, small rocks rained down on Pyrite, bouncing off his face.

"Hey! Watch where you're stepping."

But before Gem could see what Pyrite was talking about, the entire mountain started to shake. There was a horrible rumbling sound as small rocks mixed with larger boulders rolled down the mountain.

"Rockslide!" shouted Obsidian.

"Rock slide? Sounds like fun!" said Pyrite, unaware of the danger.

"No. Falling rocks! Find cover!"

They bobbed, weaved, and jumped around as the rocks crashed all around them, taking chunks of the mountain down into the clouds below.

While most of the group struggled, Gem appeared to be right at home, hopping from boulder to boulder with ease.

"Are you actually enjoying this?" asked Opal between breaths.

"What if I am?" responded Gem.

As quickly as it had started, the rockslide stopped.

As the group checked their bearings, Obsidian noticed they were surrounded by large, greenish boulders. "Nobody move."

"Why not?" asked Pyrite.

"Be quiet," said Obsidian as he stared intently at the boulders.

Then one by one, the boulders unfolded.

They unraveled to reveal brawny, rugged rock figures. Each one was covered in glowing war paint. Obsidian had a sinking feeling these warrior-like rocks were not too friendly.

Four of the rock warriors rolled forward to face the kids. As they unrolled and stood up, they introduced themselves in turn.

"I am Lherzolite!"

"I am Harzburgite!"

"I am Dunite!"

"And I am Wehrlite!" said the smallest of the four.

Then the four of them spoke together. "We are the Trap Rocks." As they continued to talk, they finished each other's sentences.

"What are—"

"you doing—"

"upon—"

"our mountain?" they asked.

"We're sorry," said Gem. "We didn't know this was

your mountain."

There was an awkward silence. "I'm Gem. This is Obsidian, Pyrite, and Opal." Another pause. "We're on a journey. Maybe you can help us?"

"We're looking for the Great Diamond," said Pyrite, trying to be helpful.

"Oh no."

"Not good."

"Kimberlite—"

"will not like that." They all shook their heads.

"Who's Kimberlite?" asked Opal.

But instead of answering her, the trap rocks rushed the group and pinned them down. There was no use fighting—they were too strong. Soon the kids were all tied together in a long rope and led forward by the rocks.

"We don't have to worry about falling now," said Pyrite, ever the optimist.

The trap rocks dragged the group further up the mountain. The climb was torturous, but soon brought them to a large opening. It was the entrance to the trap rocks' cave.

"Kimberlite—"

"will know—"

"what to—"

"do with you!" they said as they led the group into darkness.

Captivating Queen

The inside of the cave was almost pitch black. The only illumination came from tiny lanterns hanging on the walls, which were barely bright enough to make the war paint glow on the trap rocks. Opal glowed as well.

"Hey, look, you're glowing again!" commented Pyrite as he smiled.

"Really? That's what you're going to focus on?" said

Opal as she shook her head.

The captives were led into a great diamond-studded hall filled with hundreds of trap rocks. In the center of the room, a magnificent chandelier hung down from the ceiling, softly illuminating a giant throne. The diamond-studded throne reached toward the ceiling like a towering monument. Whoever, or whatever, sat there must've been colossal— much larger than any of the trap rocks they'd seen.

"I wonder if this is the home of the Great Diamond," Gem whispered to Opal. But Opal was too awed at the sight to respond.

The four guards stepped forward.

"Kimberlite!"

"Our leader!"

"Our queen!"

"Our savior!" They sang praises as they bowed in front of the throne.

Opal, Gem, Obsidian, and Pyrite looked confused.

"Are they talking to a chair?" asked Obsidian.

"Looks empty to me," said Gem.

"Maybe she's very tiny," added Pyrite.

Then the guards continued.

"We bring—"

"these trespassers—"

"these seekers—"

"of the great diamond," they all said in sequence.

For a second, there was no sound at all. Then, the

throne began to move. It slowly shook as it unfurled. The sound it made was horrible, like hundreds of shards of broken glass scraping on rocks. The throne stood even taller now as the outer shell transformed into a long cape, revealing a slender-looking figure. She was thin and pointy, and growing out of the top of her head was a magnificent crown of diamonds.

She glided effortlessly toward the captives, glaring with her cold diamond eyes.

"So," said Kimberlite. The word melted out of her mouth, much warmer and softer than they anticipated. "You've come for our diamonds."

The captives had no idea what she was talking about.

Then Queen Kimberlite moved toward the center of the hall. She raised her arms and called to her minions. "Why do they think they can climb our mountain?" The rock warriors all mumbled as she spoke. "Why do they think they can take our diamonds? Maybe they don't know how strong we are. Maybe they think we're dumb. Let's show them what happens when one tries to steal from the trap rocks!"

The trap rocks cheered.

"But we weren't—" Before Gem could finish her words, one of the guards poked at her with his spear.

"Put them in the dungeon!" commanded Kimberlite.

"I think that's Kimberlite," whispered Pyrite, proud of himself for figuring it out. Opal just shook her head.

The captives were whisked away through dark tunnels. The only illumination in the tunnels came from small holes in the ceiling that let in the moonlight. After walking through what seemed like an endless labyrinth, they were thrown into a holding cell. It was even darker in the cell, and they could barely see each other.

"What are we going to do now?" worried Pyrite.

"We'll figure something out," said Gem confidently. She found her way over to the cell door and felt around for a weak area or way to open it. But it was no use. The door would not budge.

"I guess we should've listened to Obsidian and turned back," said Pyrite as he flopped down on the floor. "I'm too young to be locked up."

"Be quiet and let us think," said Opal. "Got any smart ideas, Obsidian?"

But there was no answer.

"Obsidian? Where are you?" called Opal as she felt around the small space with her hands. But there was no sign of Obsidian.

"They took Obsidian!" cried Pyrite.

"Relax—he couldn't have gone far," said Opal, trying to calm Pyrite down.

Then they heard something.

"Pssst. Pssst!" called a voice from just outside their cell. "Are you guys okay?"

"Obsidian?" questioned Pyrite.

"What are you doing out there?" asked Opal through the door.

"Shhhh. Keep it down. I snuck away while we were in the tunnels. I was able to cut myself free using my sharp edges," said Obsidian. "I guess my darkness came in handy since no one saw me. Not even you guys."

Obsidian carefully opened the cell door from the outside, freeing his friends. "Now be quiet. We don't want the guards to hear us."

Pyrite was so excited, he gave his buddy a great big hug.

"Glad to see…you too," croaked Obsidian as Pyrite squeezed him tightly.

It was so dark in the tunnel; they couldn't see where they were going. And as Pyrite tried to get his bearings, he tripped over Opal.

"Whoa, whoa." Pyrite wobbled as he crashed to the floor.

The noise caught the attention of one of the guards. "Hey! They're escaping!" he shouted.

"Run!" shouted Gem, and they sprinted through the tunnels away from the voice. There were pools of light just ahead, and the group ran toward the light.

"We've gotta get out of these tunnels," yelled Opal.

"There," said Gem as she stopped under one of the holes that let in the moonlight. "These holes are big enough for us to escape through. And they look like they lead outside."

"Right!" said Obsidian as he looked up at the hole. "How do you suppose we get up there? And fast!"

The guards were just on their heels.

"I've got this," said Pyrite. He pulled a long rope from his backpack.

"You had a rope this entire time?" asked Obsidian furiously. "Why didn't you use it on the climb up?"

Pyrite just shrugged. "Give me your pendant."

Obsidian was reluctant to part with it. His pendant, which was an arrowhead, was a gift from his dad.

"Just do it!" shouted Gem. "They're getting closer."

Obsidian grudgingly handed the arrowhead to Pyrite, who tied it to the end of the rope. Pyrite twirled it a couple of times and tossed it up through the hole. The arrow pierced the ground above and locked into place.

"After you," said Pyrite as he held the rope.

Gem climbed up first, making it look easy. Then Opal followed right behind her, having a bit more difficulty.

Obsidian went next, and just as Pyrite started his climb, the guards were upon him.

"Pyrite!" shouted Gem and Opal from above.

Pyrite let go of the rope. He had to do something, or else the guards would capture him. He swung his arms around, scraping them against the walls. Sparks flew everywhere. Pyrite ran around in a circle, smashing and banging his arms against the walls until the sparks ignited the rope, creating smoke. The hallway was soon engulfed in a dark cloud. The guards couldn't see anything. Pyrite jumped above the burning part of the rope and climbed up. He was safe!

"That was fun!" he said breathlessly.

Pyrite quickly pulled up what was left of the rope, and put out the flames.

Obsidian pulled his treasured pendant out of the ground and placed it back around his neck. He looked ahead at the moonlit rocky landscape. "Let's get as far away from here as we can before those things find us."

Pieces of You

Gem found herself walking down a long, dark corridor lined with mineral kids on both sides. The flickering lights in the hallway buzzed in Gem's ear as they illuminated the unfriendly faces staring at her. She immediately knew that she was back in Mineral School, where she had sworn never to return. The flashing lights from the broken fixtures blinded Gem as she found herself at the center of attention. The mineral kids began to laugh and point at her. Their echoing chants of "Rock Face, Rock Face, you belong in a rock place" pushed down on her like heavy stones, making it hard for her to breathe. She was reliving her worst day.

Gem ran outside, trying to get away from the torment, but found herself in the schoolyard, surrounded by more mocking mineral kids. There was nowhere for her to escape. Then she saw him: the little zincite boy. He looked so innocent now, but a sudden rush of fear came over Gem as she remembered her scar. She knew what was about to happen. Before she could stop him, he picked the rock up off the ground and flung it. She watched as it flew through the air, as if in slow motion, and headed straight for her. She tried to run away, but her legs failed her. She was frozen with fear. Then with a loud shatter, the rock exploded violently as it made contact, cracking her shoulder.

She looked at the crack. It looked different than she remembered. It was darker, more jagged, and it was slowly growing. She realized the laughter from the children was making the crack grow. Gem looked up and saw Marble. Gem ran to Marble as she tried to get away from the laughter. But as she ran, pieces of her shoulder began to break off. Piece by piece she was falling apart. She tried to reach out to Marble but tripped as her feet and legs crumbled and turned to dust. And right before she hit the floor, Gem woke up.

She had been dreaming.

After getting away from the trap rocks, the group had made their way through the jagged mountain top, eventually growing too tired to carry on. And huddled together under a giant pillar, they had fallen asleep.

Now that Gem was awake, she was shivering. She clutched the scar on her shoulder and began to cry. All her fears and worries rose up through her and came out at once. But as she glanced around and saw the warm, peaceful faces of her sleeping new teammates, something happened inside of her. Gem felt a sudden sense of peace, a calmness that she had never felt before. She thought about everything she had been through; all the teasing, all the rejection. But with Opal, Pyrite, and Obsidian, it was different. She didn't experience any of that. It had only been a few days since they met, but it felt like a lifetime. Gem wondered if this is how it could be with everyone someday, maybe even Marble again. And the only one who could give her the answers she needed to make that happen, was the Great Diamond. She felt more determined than ever to find him. At peace after releasing her nightmares, Gem closed her eyes and quickly drifted into a serene slumber.

Everything Falls Apart

The next morning when they awoke, their surroundings were a lot more evident. It was no wonder that the trap rocks hadn't followed. The ashen landscape was covered in jutting rock pillars, and the ground was cracked and broken. They felt an eerie cold as the damp morning haze drifted past them.

"I don't like this," said Obsidian.

"Who does?" responded Opal.

As they stepped over the uneven ground, small chunks broke off and disappeared into the fog below. There was no telling what rested down there.

It wasn't long before they arrived at the edge of a cliff. It was a dead end.

"That's a long fall," said Pyrite, looking down, although he couldn't really see the bottom through the haze.

"Then let's not fall," said Opal as she pulled out her map. "These must be the Stibnite Cliffs. We're almost there, guys! The Great Diamond must be just below."

"So how do we get down?" asked Pyrite.

Gem turned to Obsidian, glaring at him. "Don't even say it!"

"What? I didn't say anything." But Obsidian was definitely thinking about turning back. The farther from home they got and the more dangers they faced, the more Obsidian wondered if he had done the right thing leaving Snowflake behind.

"Come on! Let's start climbing. We're so close!" said Gem impatiently. She was anxious to get down as quickly as possible.

As Gem stepped to the edge, the ground began to shake and plumes of steam rose from the canyon below. The steam swirled around as it drifted past them and stroked their faces. As the vapors thinned, terrible glowing eyes shined through, followed by a monstrous metallic face that was mostly teeth. It was a massive stibnite giant. Its dark, sharp, spike-covered body rose from the canyon below as it reached out with its big strong hands.

"Run!" yelled Obsidian.

"Again?" whined Pyrite.

The stibnite giant hurled shards of black, shiny stibnite at them.

"Never mind. Running is fine by me!" shouted Pyrite as he bolted away from the giant.

The group jumped around, avoiding the shards of stibnite that pierced the ground.

"Ouch!" yelled Pyrite as a piece grazed his legs.

Obsidian dodged two pieces, but a third one tore his shirt. "Ahh! My shirt. You're going to have to pay for that!" he yelled at the giant.

The stibnite giant seemed to be enjoying himself. He laughed as he pulled more spikes off his back to throw.

"Where is he getting those?" asked Opal as she ran in a zigzag to avoid the shards.

Gem dodged a piece that almost hit her head. "I think he's pulling them off his back."

"Eww! That's gross!" said Opal.

Opal, Pyrite, and Obsidian were able to run for cover under the jutting pillars, but Gem found herself trapped. She was too close to the edge. With nowhere to go, Gem decided she'd had enough.

"That's it! I've had it," she shouted. "Hey, you!

Giant monster thing. I'm not afraid of you! Now stop throwing your back spikes at us and let us pass!"

The stibnite giant stopped, lowered his head down to Gem's level, and growled, "ARRRGGGGG!" blowing Gem to the ground.

"What is that thing? And how do we stop it?" asked Obsidian frantically.

"Hey, Obsidian!" shouted Pyrite. "He's black and shiny like you! Don't you know how to stop it?" Suddenly, a mischievous thought ran through Pyrite's mind, drawing a great grin on his face. "Hey, Obsidian, maybe he's your father!"

Obsidian wasn't amused. "We have to help Gem!"

Pyrite turned to the stibnite giant, who was looming over Gem. "Hey, monster dude! Can you say, 'I'm your father?' Come on, please?"

"What are you doing?" asked Obsidian.

But the stibnite giant turned his focus from Gem. Then he repeated in a low voice, "I-I-I'm-m-m y-y-o-o-u-u-r fa-a-a-th-e-e-r-r-r."

Pyrite was extremely amused and immediately burst into laughter.

The stibnite giant, hearing Pyrite's laughter, began to laugh as well. "Huh-huh-huh." Then it repeated, "I-I-I'm-m-m y-y-o-o-o-u-u-r fa-a-a-th-e-e-e-r-r!"

"What's going on?" asked Opal.

Now Pyrite and the stibnite giant were going back and forth, saying, "I'm your father," as they laughed.

Obsidian sighed, "Really?"

But before they could relax, the stibnite giant started falling apart. He was laughing so hard that he was literally cracking up. The pieces fell all around them, and onto Gem, who was still below the creature.

"Pyrite! Stop making him laugh," yelled Obsidian. But it was too late.

As the stibnite giant fell apart, a large piece of stibnite exploded off the giant and broke the cliff where Gem stood.

Gem vanished into the canyon below.

Tears for a Friend

Gem was gone, lost in the mist. The stibnite giant was gone as well, crumbled to pieces. Opal held onto Pyrite as they both cried. Obsidian sat alone, his head lowered in his hands. *What are we going to do now?* he thought. The sky got darker as menacing gray clouds rolled in and it began to pour. But Opal, Pyrite, and Obsidian didn't even notice the large raindrops pounding down on them.

The rain cleared the mist in the canyon below. And as Obsidian looked over the edge, he could finally see the bottom of the cliff. The drop was even longer than he imagined, with stibnite spires jutting out along the entire length. The rain also created small waterfalls that skipped around on the spires and splashed into a body of water below.

"Guys, look," Obsidian pointed. "Down there. There's a lake. Maybe Gem's…" He paused, then forced the words out. "Maybe she's alive." The lake below gave him hope.

Pyrite and Opal slowly walked closer to the edge and looked down. They saw the lake below and noticed how far down Gem would have dropped.

"We have to go down there," said Obsidian. "We have to find Gem."

"Maybe we should finally turn back," said Pyrite sadly. The usually spunky friend was losing hope for the first time.

"No! We've come too far. We can't go back now, not without Gem." Obsidian felt a sense of courage that he had never experienced before. His desire to find Gem left no room for any other emotion. "We'll have to climb. We can use those stibnite spires to hold onto." Obsidian started on the descent. "Come on, stay close. And, Pyrite, give me your rope!"

Obsidian, Opal, and Pyrite grabbed hands as they made their way down, and used the rope to keep themselves together. The climb down the cliff was extremely treacherous. One wrong step and they could lose another one of their friends. And the rain made the stibnite very slippery.

They had gone down a fair distance when they ran out of spires to hold onto.

"We're going to have to jump from here," said Obsidian. They detached themselves from the rope, and Pyrite wound it and put it back in his backpack. The lake wasn't that far below. "I'll go first," said Obsidian.

Opal wanted to tell Obsidian how impressed she was with his bravery, but she didn't know how. Instead, she gave her friend a big, encouraging smile as he stepped to the edge of the rock.

Obsidian made the leap.

He flew gracefully through the air as he shut his eyes and felt the soothing wind on his face. And with a loud splash, he submerged into the water below. As he rose back up, he called to his friends with relief. "Go ahead; it's safe."

Pyrite looked scared, so Opal knew it was her turn to be brave. She grabbed his hand. "I better not get my sketchbook wet," she said. Then they both jumped down together.

An exhilarating rush ran through them as they shot down to the lake below. They sank deep into the frigid water, but quickly pushed themselves back to the surface.

"Let's do that again!" shouted Pyrite, rushing with adrenaline.

All three rested for a second next to the small lake, watching the waterfalls skip down the cliff. Opal pulled out her sketchbook from her backpack. "Whew!" she said, relieved it was still dry.

After a few moments, Obsidian started the search. "She must be down here somewhere," he said. But there was no immediate sign of his friend. He saw pieces of the Stibnite Giant spread on the ground, but the rest of him must've been at the bottom of the lake. With a shudder Obsidian wondered if maybe Gem was down there as well.

As much as he feared what he might find, he also knew what he had to do. "I'm going to search the lake," said Obsidian as he dove back into the water. He pushed himself down and swam all over the lake bottom. Pieces of broken stibnite were scattered all over the lake floor making it difficult to navigate, but there was no sign of Gem.

Opal and Pyrite were scouring the ground for any signs as well. "I don't see anything," said Opal.

"Not in the lake either," said Obsidian as he climbed back out of the water.

"That's good, right?" asked Opal. Both Pyrite and Obsidian agreed.

"Gem! Gem!" called Pyrite, hoping she would hear him. Then he stepped on something. "Ow!" cried Pyrite.

"You okay?" asked Obsidian.

"I think so. Just stepped on this rock," he said, picking it up. He was about to toss it into the lake, when Opal stopped him.

"Wait! Let me look at that." She rushed over and grabbed the rock out of Pyrite's hand. "It's Gem," she said as she studied it.

"What?" said Pyrite. "That's not Gem. She's much bigger."

"No, it's a piece of her. This rock, it's exactly like Gem. And look, parts of her scar." Opal rubbed her finger over the grooves in the rock, but it crumbled in her hands. "It must've broken off when she fell."

"Where's the rest of her?" asked Pyrite, looking confused.

As they looked around, Obsidian noticed a small alley tucked between two cliff walls. It seemed like the only path that didn't lead to the lake. "Come on; maybe she went that way."

The three of them walked through the narrow path, the cliff walls brushing their shoulders.

"I have to find her," said Obsidian to himself.

"It's not your fault," said Opal, trying to comfort him. "It was her decision to come out here. Plus, if I hadn't told her about the Great Diamond, none of us would be here either."

"No, it's my fault," said Pyrite. "If I hadn't made that giant laugh, she wouldn't have fallen."

"Let's just find her," said Obsidian.

The path got wider as they walked. They were no longer squeezed between the cliff walls. But they soon came to a dead end.

"Now what?" said Pyrite. "No sign of Gem anywhere."

But the cliffside told Opal a different story.

Dead End

Opal quickly pulled the map out of her backpack. "Look!" she said as she pointed. "Diamond Canyon."

Carved on the side of the cliff was a giant dragon just like on her map. And positioned on its chest was the most perfect diamond they had ever seen.

"Is that a real dragon?" asked Pyrite.

"No, it looks like a carving. Probably here to scare

off anyone searching for the Great Diamond," said Opal.

"I'd say it's working," said Pyrite, looking frightened by the menacing dragon. "I feel like it's looking at me."

"Look around—there's got to be a lever or a secret passage out of here," commanded Obsidian.

They looked around but found no way out; it was just a dead end.

Then as Obsidian was staring up at the dragon, he had an idea. "I think that diamond on its chest is a key. I bet if we push it, a door opens somewhere. That's how it always works in stories."

"Here," he said as he put his hands together for Pyrite to step on. "I'll help you climb up."

"Climb that?" blurted Pyrite. "But, but, it's a dragon."

"Come on, it's just a statue." Obsidian boosted Pyrite up and onto the dragon. "Opal and I will stay down here and look out for anything that opens."

Pyrite reluctantly climbed the dragon.

"Did you reach it?" asked Opal.

As Pyrite approached the dragon's chest, he could see the dragon's giant eyes staring down at him. "This is not cool," he said to himself.

"Just press on it," yelled Obsidian from below.

Pyrite lightly placed his fingers on the diamond, and just as he was about to push on it, the dragon lowered its head.

"Ahhh!" shouted Pyrite. "I knew it was real!"

He dashed back down as the dragon began to emerge from the cliffside.

Obsidian and Opal stared in disbelief as the creature ripped its wings off the cliffside.

"Hurry!" shouted Obsidian as he held his arms out for Pyrite.

Pyrite jumped off the dragon, and just as he landed in Obsidian's arms, the dragon extended one of its feet and grabbed Pyrite and Obsidian with its claws. Then it broke another foot free and grabbed hold of Opal.

The dragon freed itself from the cliffside, flapped its wings, and soared into the sky.

"Great idea, Obsidian!" said Pyrite as he dangled in the air.

The dragon carried them through the clouds, gently clenching them in its claws. Before long they approached a tall, narrow tower that poked through the clouds. The dragon glided down and dropped them on top of the tower before vanishing back into the clouds.

They were relieved to be free from the dragon, but worried about how they were going to get down from the tower. And if they were ever going to find Gem.

"That dragon, maybe it brought Gem here as well," said Obsidian optimistically.

"Look, over there," said Opal, pointing to a small door. Like the dragon, it was carved into the wall.

"Maybe it's an elevator," said Pyrite.

Opal rolled her eyes at her friend, though she was

truly glad to see his spirits were at least rising.

"Let's see if we can open it," said Obsidian.

The door was heavy and took the strength of all three of them to open. Behind the door was a spiral staircase that looked like it went on forever. With no other viable options, they started to descend the stairs. The walls were studded with small rocks and minerals—thousands of them—sparkling in every color imaginable.

"This is amazing!" said Opal. "I've never seen so many different kinds of rocks and minerals. And, look, they're all labeled."

Each rock and mineral had a small tag under it.

Blood Opal
Chalcedony
Bornite
Skarn
Carnelian
Pegmatite
Baryte
Cryolite

It looked like a museum. Opal wanted to stop and sketch all the rocks and minerals, but there were just too many. Plus, she wanted to find Gem more. The three of them made their way down the staircase.

"Come on, I see another door," said Obsidian.

This door was much lighter, and Obsidian was able to push it open easily. As he peeked inside, he saw a dark figure looming over someone.

Is that Gem? thought Obsidian.

Diamond in the Rough

I t's Gem!" shouted Obsidian as he dashed over to her. "Get away from her!" he yelled to the figure. Pyrite and Opal ran in after Obsidian.

But before Obsidian could get to Gem, a large dark beast lunged at him. It was massive. Obsidian froze in his tracks as Pyrite and Opal crashed into his back. The old gray graphite dog stared them down.

"Alpha, down, boy," called the figure inside. The old

gray dog quickly plopped onto the ground, sighed, and fell asleep.

"Sorry about Alpha. He's very protective," said an old man who slowly revealed himself. He was short and walked with a cane, his body mostly covered by a dark gray shawl.

"What have you done to Gem?" Obsidian demanded.

"Gem. So that's her name," said the old figure. "What a great name."

Gem appeared to be asleep.

"Crystal brought her here," said the old figure. "Just like she brought all of you here. Your friend is unconscious and needs to rest. What happened to her?"

"She fell," said Pyrite.

"Standing up to a stibnite giant," added Opal.

"I see," said the old man. "That must be how she hurt her shoulder. I did what I could to mend it."

Obsidian walked over and sat down next to Gem. She was covered by a large soft blanket. She looked very peaceful lying there with her eyes closed.

Pyrite whispered to Opal. "Any idea who he is?"

Opal studied the old man carefully. His pale blue eyes were wise and sincere looking. And although his transparent face was cloudy and warn, the facets in his beard sparkled as they split the light into a rainbow of colors.

Suddenly, she realized who he was.

"You're the Great Diamond, aren't you?" said Opal.

The old man was amused. "Ha! The Great Diamond! The Great Diamond." He repeated the name to himself over and over. "No one's called me that in a long time."

"So it is you!" exclaimed Opal.

The Great Diamond nodded. After everything they had been through, it was hard to believe they had finally found him…an old man hidden away from the world.

"And your leg, that's from the explosion, isn't it?" Opal followed up.

"That it is," said the Great Diamond as he tapped his leg with his cane. "Seems as though you know a lot more about me than I know about you. Tell me, what are you kids doing here, this far away from the village?"

"We've been on a journey to find you," said Obsidian. He grabbed the map from Opal before she could pull it away. "This map showed us the way."

The Great Diamond looked at the map and asked, "Where did you get this?"

Opal stepped up. "It was my mom's. She was a big fan of yours, studied all your works. I don't know where she got the map, but she always wanted to find you."

"Interesting," said the Great Diamond as he walked over to take a closer look at Opal. "You're the second mineral I've handed this map to. The first one must've been your mom."

Opal was shocked. She couldn't believe what she was hearing. "You mean my mom found you? She was here?"

"Indeed," said the Great Diamond. "I gave her the map so she would know what areas to avoid. But I had her promise that she would never tell anyone that she found me. Sounds like she kept her promise."

"This map shows landmarks to avoid?" asked Opal.

"That's correct, why?" said the Great Diamond.

Opal didn't know what to say. She felt confused, shocked, lost, and embarrassed. She had been mistaken about the map. She had been misled about her mother's quest. Opal wondered why her mother had kept such a big secret from her.

The Great Diamond continued, "That still doesn't explain what you're doing here."

Obsidian looked down at Gem. "We're here because of her. She was desperate to find you, to ask you a question."

"You came all this way so she could ask me a question?" said the Great Diamond. "Poor girl. She got hurt because of me."

Opal stepped in. "She wanted to know why she was born different. Why she's was born a rock, when her parents are minerals." Opal's voice dropped. "And when I told her about the Great...about you, and how you know everything, she was determined to find you."

"I definitely don't know everything," said the Great Diamond humbly.

All the talking made Gem stir.

"She's waking up!" exclaimed Obsidian.

Hidden Gems

Gem slowly pulled herself up, still dazed from her fall. And as the blanket slipped off her shoulder, Opal, Obsidian, and Pyrite saw the extent of her damage for the first time.

Obsidian kneeled down to his waking friend. Gem could see the worry in his eyes.

"What is it?" she asked.

But before Obsidian could answer, Gem noticed

her reflection on Obsidian's dark surface. She turned to look. The top of her shoulder was missing. The scar she had was gone, and in its place remained a large hole.

But the hole wasn't hollow. It was densely packed with purple amethyst crystals of varying sizes. It was the most frightening and beautiful thing Gem had ever seen.

"Don't be alarmed, Gem," said the Great Diamond. "You're going to be just fine."

Gem looked at the Great Diamond, confused as to who he was. Then she glanced around the room. "Where am I? Who is he?"

Opal bent down to Gem. "We made it, Gem. We found the Great Diamond."

It was all too much for Gem; she didn't know what to say.

The Great Diamond turned to Gem. "Your friends say that you have a question for me."

All the questions Gem ever had about her life and her parents and about being a rock or a mineral rushed through her mind. She still couldn't process it all.

"I did. But, now…" She glanced at the minerals in her shoulder.

"You probably want some answers about that," said the Great Diamond.

Finally, Gem was able to speak. "I…I don't know. I don't know what to think anymore. Until today, I wanted to know why I was born a rock," she said, her words coming quickly now. "Why I didn't belong, didn't fit in. And now, look at me: What am I? A rock? A mineral?" Gem shut her eyes as she tried to hide from the world.

The Great Diamond slowly bent down to Gem's level as Gem opened her eyes. The Great Diamond smiled. "You're both," he said softly. "Gem, you're a geode."

Pyrite gasped in awe. "Whoa!" Then he turned to Opal. "What's a geode?"

The Great Diamond heard Pyrite's question. "Ah, geodes are special. Special indeed." The Great Diamond stood back up. "Geodes are rock on the outside, but mineral on the inside. Most geodes never find out what they truly are. They live their entire lives without discovering the complexity and beauty inside. Gem, you're one of the lucky ones."

Gem didn't feel very lucky as thoughts began to race through her mind. She started to worry about all the rocks and minerals back home. Where would she fit in now? Where does someone who is both rock and mineral belong? She worried that she'd have to leave the village like the old lady Celest.

The Great Diamond could see the worry on Gem's face. "What's the matter, Gem?"

Gem pulled herself away from her own thoughts. "Where do I belong now? With the rocks, or the minerals?"

The Great Diamond laughed. "Rocks! Minerals! What's the difference!"

Opal stepped in. "What do you mean? Everyone knows you are either a rock or a mineral."

"And who do you think decided that?" asked the Great Diamond. "Who do you think put everyone in nice little groups so they could be studied?" He tapped his cane on his bad leg. "It's one of my biggest mistakes. I never stopped to think of the consequences labeling everything would have."

"You mean *you* divided the rocks and minerals?" asked Gem. Her initial wonder had now turned into anger.

"I'm afraid so," said the Great Diamond. "And that mistake has haunted me for a lifetime. I can't change the past, but maybe I can change the future."

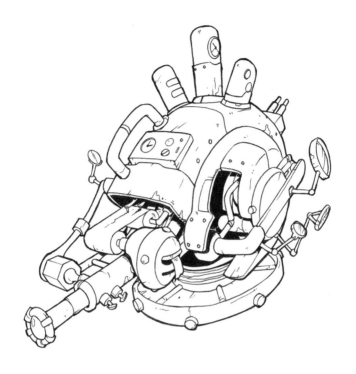

Knowledge Will Set You Free

G em couldn't believe what she was hearing. All this effort, putting her new friends in danger, and for what? To seek out the one mineral who had caused all her strife to begin with? He was to blame for all the pain she felt, for making her feel so alone. Now she knew what Celest meant when she said, "It's all his fault."

"Let me try to explain," said the Great Diamond

as he gestured to the rock-and-mineral-studded walls. "What do you think rocks are made out of?" he asked.

No one had an answer, not even Opal.

The Great Diamond pointed to one of the rocks on the wall. "Who knows what that is?" he asked.

Opal knew the rock well. "That's granite," she said flatly.

"Correct," replied the Great Diamond. "But what is granite?" he asked.

No one felt like getting a lesson from him now.

"What do you mean?" asked Opal. "Granite is granite; it's a rock."

The Great Diamond laughed. "It's not so simple." He walked over to a large golden machine with metal arms and glass disks.

"Do you know why I left the village? It was because of this," he said, tapping on the machine with his cane. "The first time I tried to build this machine, it didn't go so well. As soon as I turned it on, the whole thing exploded. It destroyed my entire lab, shattered my leg, and even hurt some folks who were near the lab."

The Great Diamond slowly shook his head, "I couldn't allow something like that ever to happen again. I couldn't risk hurting anyone else, or even worse. So I packed my stuff and left. I wandered until I found a place that I could be sure was far enough away that no one would get hurt."

The Great Diamond flipped through the disks as he

assembled them. He had about six glass disks stacked on top of each other, which created a microscope with surprising strength. He grabbed the granite from the wall and placed it in the X-ray chamber of the machine. Then he flipped the switch. The machine roared and beeped and lit up.

"After years of tinkering, I finally perfected it. Now it's safe to use. See for yourself," said the Great Diamond.

Still reluctant but curious, Opal went first. She stared through the glass disks. She couldn't believe her eyes. She no longer saw granite.

"Is that quartz?" Opal asked. "And mica?" Nothing was as it seemed.

"Very good," replied the Great Diamond. He pressed a button on the machine, that triggered a flash of light and a printout on a small piece of paper. He handed the paper to Opal. As she read it, it confirmed what she had seen with her eyes, and more.

"Quartz, mica, plagioclase," read Opal.

Pyrite and Obsidian squeezed in to get a look. They could see small pieces of different minerals. What looked like a single rock without the glass disks, now looked like multiple minerals.

"It's taken me a long time to discover the truth, but most rocks are made of minerals," said the Great Diamond.

Gem still couldn't believe what she was hearing.

Then she thought about her old friend. "What about marble?" she asked.

The Great Diamond looked to his walls and found a small marble specimen. He took the granite out of the machine and replaced it with the piece of marble. "Take a look."

Gem stood up and slowly walked over to the machine. She placed the glass disks over the marble. She could see small white crystals. "What are those?"

"Calcite crystals," noted the Great Diamond. "Marble is usually mostly calcite, mixed with other minerals." He triggered the button that released the printout, "this one's composed of calcite and graphite."

Gem couldn't believe it. Her entire life, she had thought that rocks and minerals were completely different. But now, those differences disappeared before her eyes.

Pyrite got excited; he wanted to see what he was made of.

"Oooh, can I try it?" He grabbed the machine and swung it over his hand. Pyrite stared at the small glass disks. "What is that?" he asked.

He moved aside as the Great Diamond looked closely at the disks. "You're mostly made out of Pyrite, which is no surprise," he said plainly. "But you also have some gold in you."

Pyrite couldn't believe his ears. All these years he'd been ashamed of being a pyrite, being called fool's gold, but he actually had gold in him. He quickly ran over to see the printout to confirm it was true, and indeed it was. He tore the printout, hugged it, and slipped it into his pocket.

Then the Great Diamond continued, "Good thing you don't have too much gold in you. Pyrite is a lot stronger."

Now Opal was interested in finding out what she was made from. She swung the machine over her arm and looked closely at the glass disks. She could see small beads. "What are those?" she asked.

"Those beads are what give you your colorful iridescence," said the Great Diamond. "Opals don't have a crystal structure like other minerals."

"Hey, Obsidian, give it a try," said Pyrite.

But Obsidian was hesitant. "I don't know," he said. He was worried about what he would discover. But with more urging from Pyrite, Obsidian swung the device over his arm. When they looked through the glass disks, they couldn't see anything.

"I didn't do it," said Pyrite, worried that he had damaged the machine.

But the Great Diamond laughed. "You didn't break the machine. You're not going to see anything with Obsidian there. Just like Opal, he doesn't have a crystal structure. But he doesn't have a beaded structure either. Obsidian is like liquid in suspended animation. That's what makes him so solid and sharp."

Obsidian wasn't quite sure what to think. But he was pleased by the thought of being solid and sharp. It made him feel more heroic.

Finally, it was Gem's turn. She hesitantly grabbed the glass disks and placed them over her shoulder. It was hard for her to see, but Opal, Pyrite, and Obsidian all gathered to look. The bright purple amethyst crystals sparkled along with the clear quartz underneath them. Gem pressed the button as the machine flashed and quickly analyzed her and gave a printout.

Gem grabbed the printout. "Quartz, amethyst, plagioclase, pyroxene." She wasn't just one mineral, she was four. Quartz like her father. Amethyst like her mother. But she was more. She was more complex than she ever imagined.

The Great Diamond noticed Opal scribbling away in her sketchbook. "Here, take this." He grabbed a giant book from his desk and handed it over to Opal. She flipped it open and shuffled through the pages.

"I've been studying rocks and minerals for a long time," said the Great Diamond. "I've documented all my findings in this book, and I've come to one conclusion. The only difference between rocks and minerals, between all of us, is the way we are formed and shaped by the world around us. We've been defined by what we look like, by our physical appearances. But the way we look doesn't define who we are, just where we've been. Deep inside, we are so much more."

"I wish everyone in the village knew about this. Then maybe they would stop caring about what I am, and see the real me," said Gem.

The Great Diamond looked at Obsidian, Opal, and Pyrite and said, "It looks like you have three amazing friends here who don't care what you are." Then he turned to Opal. "Take that book with you and share what you have learned here today with the village. Maybe they're finally ready to hear the truth."

"What if they don't believe us?" asked Opal.

The Great Diamond thought for a second. "I have an idea. Seeing is believing."

The Flight Home

The sun was starting to sink once again as they all stepped out on top of the tower. The Great Diamond strapped the golden metal machine to Crystal, who would be flying them home. The group was grateful that they wouldn't have to face the treacherous forest again.

Once they all climbed aboard, the Great Diamond turned to Opal, Gem, Obsidian, and Pyrite. "You are all very brave," he said. "Braver than I was. I started something that tore rocks and minerals apart, and never undid what I started. But because of your bravery, maybe they can finally come together again."

The kids nodded to the old man. They understood now why he had hidden away, and they hoped that sharing their newfound knowledge would bring him and the entire village some peace.

Just as they were about to leave, Opal remembered something. "Hey, Pyrite, didn't you have a question to ask as well?"

Pyrite thought about it for a second. "Why do they call you the Grand, I mean, the Great Diamond?"

"*That's* your question?" said Opal as she crossed her arms. But she was secretly even more interested in the answer than Pyrite.

Just as the Great Diamond was about to explain, Crystal flapped her large wings and jumped off the tower.

"This is awesome!" shouted Pyrite as they launched into the sky and soared through the air.

They passed by the stibnite giant, who had assembled himself back together. He waved at them as he roared, "I'm-m-m-m y-y-y-o-o-o-u-u-r fa-a-a-a-th-e-e-r."

Then they passed over the trap rocks, who hurled spears at them that fell short.

They flew over Mercury Lake and zipped by Ruby

and Moonstone.

"Looks like they found our father!" said Ruby.

They waved as they glided by Mrs. Tiger's Eye and her cubs, and old lady Celest with her toxic mineral babies. Finally, they passed over the river with the tumblers, who were still tumbling away.

As they arrived home, the entire village—both rocks and minerals—gathered around to see the children flying in on the back of a dragon.

Gem stood on top of Crystal to greet the village. She took a deep breath. "I'm Gem, and these are my friends Opal, Pyrite, and Obsidian. And we have just returned from a journey to find the Great Diamond."

Murmurs rose up from the crowd about the mysterious Great Diamond, who many had forgotten.

Gem continued, "For far too long, we have lived as either rocks or minerals. But now, thanks to the Great Diamond, we know the truth." Gem looked at her new friends standing tall next to her. "Those labels don't make us who we are; they only divide us. We are more than what we look like on the surface. Deep inside, we are all made from the same things. Come, see for yourselves. This machine can show you what you're made from. From this day forward, let's stop being afraid of our differences, and instead, celebrate what makes each one of us unique."

One by one the crowd began to step forward, intrigued by the elaborate golden machine.

Opal jumped down with the Great Diamond's book in her hand. She was ready to share it with anyone who would listen.

"Opal!" shouted a voice. It was Opal's dad. He raced to her and gave her a big hug. "I was so worried about you. Don't ever leave like that again!"

"Don't worry, Dad, I'm fine," said Opal, struggling to hold onto the book with one hand.

"What's that?" asked her dad.

"This? Um, it's a book, from the Great Diamond."

"You're just like your mom," he said as he squeezed her tighter.

Opal wondered if her dad knew more than he let on.

"Obsidian!" yelled a little voice. It was Snowflake, standing with their mom.

Obsidian ran to his little sister and picked her up and hugged her. "Were you good for Mom?" he asked.

"Yup!" answered Snowflake proudly.

"Glad to see you're okay," said Obsidian's mom. "And by the way, you're grounded."

Pyrite heard his name. It was Beryl, and he was standing with Pyrite's parents.

"Welcome back, little Pyrite. Your parents came back a bit early."

Mr. Pyrite stepped forward. "So, I see you went on an adventure of your own. Why didn't you tell us you wanted to go on adventures? We would've taken you along on ours."

Pyrite was confused. He never imagined his parents would want him tagging along on their trips.

"Guess what, Dad?" said Pyrite excitedly as he pulled the printout from his pocket. "I have gold in me! Real gold!"

"That's not a surprise," said Mr. Pyrite, looking at the piece of paper. "Your great-grandmother was pure gold."

Pyrite couldn't believe his ears. He put his arms around his parents. "Tell me more!"

Gem was about to jump down from Crystal. She had been taking in the scene from above, hopeful for a change that would allow her and her outcast friends to feel welcome. As she patted Crystal on the head and thanked her, she heard a familiar voice.

A Long Story

I'm sorry, Gem," said a faint voice from below. Gem looked down to see her old friend Marble. She looked so small and delicate, just like when they had first met. Marble's pale-gray eyes stared regretfully as she looked up at Gem. Marble wasn't sure how Gem was going to react to seeing her after what she had done.

"I don't know what came over me. Everything is

so confusing these days, but I know what I did was wrong," said Marble as she began to tear up. "Will you ever forgive me?"

Gem's heart swelled up with uncontrolled emotion. Before Marble could say another word, Gem jumped down and gave Marble the biggest hug she had ever given.

After Gem finally let go, Marble suddenly noticed Gem's shoulder. "What happened to you?" exclaimed Marble as she danced her fingers over the exposed amethyst crystals.

"I fell," said Gem, laughing. "But I'm okay, better then okay actually."

"Must have been some fall," said Marble. "I guess you really are a mineral."

"It complicated," teased Gem, repeating the exact words Marble had spoken to her before.

Gem pulled out the jasper flower she had stored away in her pocket and handed it to Marble. "Here, I saved this for you."

Marble grabbed the jasper flower and gave Gem another big hug. "Thank you," said Marble as she stuck the red flower into her white hair. She realized that Gem had never given up on her.

"Come on, I have to show you something. It's going to blow your mind!" said Gem as she dragged Marble by the arm. But as they ran toward the machine, Gem saw her parents.

"Gem!" called her mom. "Where have you been? We were so worried."

But before Gem could answer, her dad noticed her shoulder. "And what happened to your shoulder!" he said, looking shocked.

"It's a long story," said Gem. "I'll tell you all about it when we get home. But don't worry, I'm fine. For the first time in my life, I know what I am."

"And what's that?" asked her mom.

"I'm Gem!"

The End.

About the Author

Hagop Kane Boughazian is a writer, director, and animator. For the past 20 years, Kane has been creating award-winning 3d computer animations for commercials, video games, music videos, short films, and the life-sciences industry.

Two years in the making, *Hidden Gems: Quest for the Great Diamond*, is Kane's debut children's novel. Inspired by his son's rock and mineral collection, Kane started telling bedtime stories to his kids about characters made of rocks and minerals. And with the help of his kids, these stories soon took on a life of their own, and a world much larger and more fantastic than Kane could have ever imagined was born – the world of Hidden Gems.

Kane lives in sunny California with his wonderful wife, and two amazing children – whose birthstones are ruby and moonstone.

Continue the adventure

www.greatdiamondpress.com

Explore the **Full Color Glossary**

Download **Coloring Pages**

Listen to the **Songs**

Watch the **Trailer**

and more!

We hope you enjoyed this book.
We would love an honest online review, or a mention on
social media, to help spread the word.

Amethyst	Baryte	Basalt	Beryl
Blood Opal	Bornite	Breccia	Brochantite
Calcite	Carnelian	Celestite	Chalcanthite
Chalcedony	Cinnabar	Citrine	Copper
Cryolite	Diamond	Dunite	Emerald
Fluorite	Galena	Garnet	Gold

Granite

Graphite

Harzburgite

Heliotrope

Hematite

Hutchinsonite

Jadeite

Jasper

Kimberlite

Labradorite

Lapis Lazuli

Lherzolite

Limestone

Malachite

Marble

Mercury

Mica

Moonstone

Natrolite

Obsidian

Opal

Pegmatite

Peridot

Plagioclase